River Daughter

Also by

JANE HARDSTAFF

The Executioner's Daughter

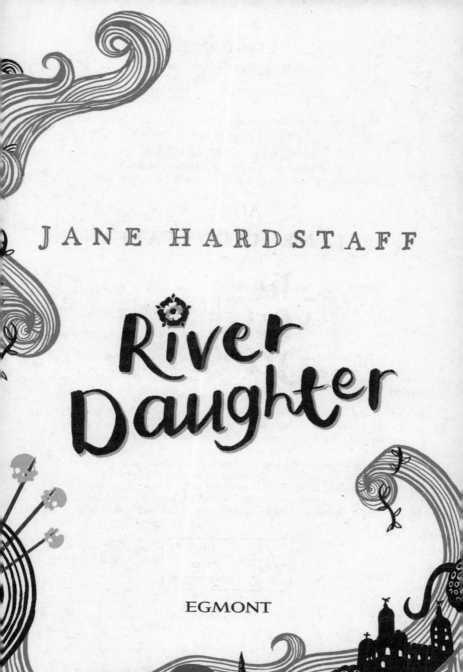

JANE HARDSTAFF

River Daughter

EGMONT

EGMONT

We bring stories to life

First published in Great Britain in 2015 by Egmont UK Limited
The Yellow Building, 1 Nicholas Road, London W11 4AN

Text copyright © 2015 Jane Hardstaff
Illustrations copyright © 2015 Joe McLaren
The moral rights of the author and illustrator have been asserted

ISBN 978 1 4052 6832 5

www.egmont.co.uk

1 3 5 7 9 10 8 6 4 2

A CIP catalogue record for this title is available from the British
Library

55868/1

Typeset by Avon DataSet Ltd, Bidford on Avon, Warwickshire
Printed and bound in Great Britain by CPI Group

MIX
Paper
FSC   FSC® C018306

For Frea

CONTENTS

CHAPTER ONE
Strange Fish

'Sweet Harry's scabs! Yer like a frog with hair, Leatherboots.'

'Bet you've never seen a frog do this!'

Moss dived down, turning a full somersault as she went, leaving Salter grinning on the riverbank. As she stretched to touch the stony river bed, she felt the drag of the water against her body. The river here was in no hurry. No roar, no raging currents, just a wide bend and a grassy bank that ushered the moorhens politely on their way. Moss knew this stretch of river as well as she knew the scratches on her knees. She knew the vole holes. She knew where the kingfishers flicked their jewel wings. She knew every dip in the river bed. Because it was here she'd learnt to swim.

She wore an old apple sack with holes cut for her neck and arms. At first Moss had gasped at the clumsiness of her kicks, fists gripped tight to the branch that kept her afloat, her friend never more than a few steps away. On the surface was a spluttering fight for air. Yet under the water, the quietness calmed her. So Salter had tied a rope around her middle and she'd let herself sink, eyes open, arms outstretched, and gradually her legs had learned a rhythm that propelled her body forward. When she ran out of breath, she would rise to the surface and gulp another. And if she strayed too far into the river, Salter would haul her back on the end of his rope like a strange fish.

Now the rope was off. More than a year had passed since she, Pa and Salter had left London, and though Salter said she frightened the trout, Moss had spent much of those summer months swimming the river.

There were times when Moss could barely believe how different this new life was to their old. All those years in the Tower of London, the taunts of the Tower folk, the thump of the drum on Execution Day, Pa standing on the scaffold with his axe in his hands. And Moss herself, holding her wretched basket ready to catch a rolling head. Just thinking about it made the bile rise from her stomach. How many hours had she spent gazing from the battlements of the Tower, willing the mighty river Thames to carry her away from that miserable life? The river *had* saved her, thought Moss. But it had almost killed her too.

A breeze rustled the leaves on the willow. Autumn was coming and it would soon be too cold for dipping. She stared down at her feet, curled against the stones of the river bed. This was a very different river to the Thames. Here the water was clear and waist deep. The only place for fish to hide was among the water crowfoot, giant green ribbons that swayed with the flow. But Moss avoided the tangled weeds and the clutch of anything that might drag her down.

Salter was lying in the grass, his dirt-smudged face propped on his elbows.

It hadn't been easy for the river boy to leave London or his beloved shack on the banks of the Thames. It had been his home, where he'd fished and thieved and managed to stay warm, winter after winter. But from the moment he'd first hauled a near-drowned Moss into his boat, their lives had changed. Though he would never admit it, they now had something that neither of them wanted to lose.

They were friends.

He was watching her now.

'Do you have to go right to the middle?' he called. 'Those great hooves'll scare the fish all the way to Silbury!'

'Don't worry about me, Smudgeface!'

'I ain't worried about you! I'm fishin later. Just don't want me catch driven away that's all.'

Moss grinned. 'Well, catch this, fisher boy!' She ducked under and swam to the bank, bobbing up in front of Salter's face with a splash.

'See.'

'I don't see nothin.'

'I can swim, or hadn't you noticed?'

She could see his smile coming. A little crows-feet crinkle in the corner of his eyes. She flipped a handful of water at his face and ducked back down, kicking strong strokes back out into the river. But when her head broke the surface, Salter wasn't looking at her any more. He was staring downriver.

'Hey!' she called, 'Come on in!'

He stood up, still peering into the distance.

'What is it?' she said.

'Dunno.'

Moss waded a few paces to the middle of the river where she had a clear view past the bend. She screwed up her eyes and stared.

There *was* something.

A dark ripple, moving slowly towards her. In front of it, specks of silver darted from the river to the bank, lightning quick, threading the grass with a shining mesh.

'What *is* that?' said Moss.

Salter squinted into the sunlight. 'Pope's earholes! It's the fish!'

'Fish?'

'The fish are jumpin. Out of the river.'

Moss stared at the bizarre sight before her. Salter was right. Driven forward by the dark ripple in the water, the fish seemed to be panicking. Leaping high out of the river and throwing themselves on to the banks. Landing in a silver heap where they gasped and jerked, helpless in the grass. She watched, mesmerised by the jumping fish and by the strange shape behind them, getting closer and closer.

'Fish leapin to their deaths . . .' Salter was shaking his head. 'Ain't never seen nothin like it.'

'It's like they can't stand to be in the water,' said

Moss. 'Like they can't get out fast enough.'

Salter jumped, as though someone had whacked the back of his head.

'Get out of the water. *Now*!'

'What?'

'Don't argue, Leatherboots! Do as I say. Quick!'

Moss dived down again, her arms pulling against the current. But something was wrong. She'd hardly moved.

'Swim!' Salter's muffled voice yelled above her.

There was a splash. Salter was still shouting. 'I'm comin! Keep swimmin, Leatherboots! Don't stop!'

All at once Moss's eyes filled with silt. She spluttered to the surface and saw Salter in the river, staggering towards her. The water was thickening with mud. It pressed in on her body, slowing her arms and legs. She tried to reach down with her feet to touch the solid river bed, but it was gone. In its place was shifting mud that oozed between her toes. All around her, the river was brown and choking, a muddy rag stuffed down its throat.

'Don't stop!' Salter was still yelling, 'Keep goin!'

But her feet wouldn't move. The mud gripped her, warm and sticky, holding her fast.

'Salter! I'm stuck!'

'Wait!' He lunged forward, arm outstretched. As if in some slow dream, Moss watched the water drag him under.

'SALTER!'

He was gone.

Now the mud beneath her began to tug at her feet. Sucking her down. Inch by inch. And the more she thrashed, the deeper she sank. Her flailing arms beat the surface to brown froth as her head was pulled slowly under.

Something brushed against her body. Through the stew of water she saw lashing fronds of water crowfoot, felt it against her legs, coiling and tightening. But instead of dragging her further down, the crowfoot seemed to be pulling upwards, as though trying to free her from the mud. Then a mighty rush of current snatched her up and she felt herself bowl over and over until all at once it stopped. Her feet found the stony river bed and she pushed with all the force she could muster, exploding to the surface in choking breaths.

On the opposite side of the river, Salter was heaving himself towards the bank.

The mud had gone. The water was clear, the crowfoot swaying gently, great, trailing tendrils, stretching towards her. She kicked out for the bank and the crowfoot seemed to pull back. But as it did, a shadow curled underneath. Too big for a fish.

For a flit of a second, the shadow showed itself. In the tangle of weeds.

What she saw almost stopped her heart.

A hand. Then a face. Then it was gone.

Moss dived back into the river, floundering through the weed, dragging it out in great clumps, pulling it apart.

Nothing. The shadow had vanished, and with it, the face.

It was a face she'd never seen before. Yet it was

familiar. Green eyes, a tangle of hair. So like her own. But older, sadder.

She couldn't be sure. She'd never seen her.

Her mother's face.

CHAPTER TWO
Old Lives, New Lives

It was dusk by the time Moss and Salter made it back to the village. She had stashed her apple sack in the hollow of the willow as usual, changing back into her dry dress in the bushes. Salter was wet through. But despite his sodden clothes, he kept up a cheery banter all the way from the fields to the lane. Every time Moss tried to mention the river, he changed the subject, so in the end she gave up and slunk into her own thoughts. In her head, a picture shimmered. She'd only seen it for a moment. But she *had* seen it.

The face. Her mother's face? Was it possible? But her mother was dead. Could that have been her spirit in the river today? She turned the thought over and over. A year and a half ago, she'd seen with her own eyes how the dead could be given life by the cold waters. The Riverwitch had revealed herself. A restless spirit who haunted the rivers, looking for children to snatch.

Ignoring Pa's pleas to stay away from the river, Moss had left him and made her way out of the Tower. And on Moss's twelfth birthday the Riverwitch had come for her, just as she'd promised on the day Moss was born. She'd dragged Moss down to the depths of the murky Thames. But there in the swirl and suck of the river, Moss succeeded in changing her fate. And the Riverwitch had let her go.

Moss, Pa and Salter had walked away from their old lives in London and settled in a country village where Pa was welcomed as the new blacksmith. During those early days, Moss had wondered whether the Witch would come for her again. But the more she'd swum in the gentle village river, the bolder she'd become, until the strangeness of that winter had seemed so far away it was almost unreal. She'd buried those memories deep, hoping she'd never have to dig them up. The Riverwitch was gone from their thoughts and their lives. But today . . . what had she seen? The coiling weeds had filled her head with thoughts of the Witch. Yet the face in the water was not the face of the Riverwitch.

The squat little forge was a welcome sight. Moss pushed at the door. Warmth and smoke wrapped her like a blanket. Pa was already asleep, a rising, falling bundle on his pallet. They trod past him softly and settled on the low stools by the fire. The clear October sky brought a chill to the air and Pa allowed a log or two to burn way into the night.

'Rabbitin tomorrow,' said Salter. 'Set the traps yesterday an' I'm goin back to see what I've got first light.'

'Salter . . .'

'Yep?'

'What *was* that, in the river?'

'Search me. Some sort of freak current. Ain't never seen it like that. All whipped up with mud an' stinkin like a badger's bum. Best not go swimmin fer a while, Leatherboots. Too dangerous. This time we was lucky.'

But it didn't feel like luck to Moss. It felt like the river had changed. And the face in the waterweed – she couldn't stop thinking about it.

'Salter,'

'Mmm.'

'Can I ask you something?'

'If you must. I can tell that head of yers is stewin. Though if you was to ask me, I'd say that questions only lead to more questions an' don't make yer troubles go away.'

Moss gave the fire a poke. On the one hand, she liked the way Salter just got on with life, making the best of things wherever possible. But he never questioned why things were the way they were, and this frustrated her no end. She supposed he couldn't help it. After all, he'd been just six years old when his parents died. From that day on, alone, with nothing but his hands and his wits, he'd had to fend for himself. 'Bread first, then morals,' he always said. Survival was the most important thing and Salter had learned not to ask too many questions, of himself or anyone else. But the village was a world away from that harsh life, thought Moss. And there were moments when she wondered if there was more to Salter than he was letting on.

'You think too much,' he said.

'Do I? And what about you? What goes on in that head of yours? Or is just full of rabbits?'

Salter grinned. 'Yep. Fish an' rabbits, that's me, shore girl.'

'*Shore* girl? I can swim almost as well as you.'

'All thanks to my brilliant teachin.'

'Oh, is that what you call it? Holding a rope and shouting from the bank?'

'I could have just thrown you in and watched you sink.'

'Do you know, sometimes I can't quite believe it. All this. Swimming in the river, us living here, Pa working the forge. It's more than I could ever have hoped for.'

Salter eyed her. 'So what's on yer mind, then?'

Moss hesitated, not even sure herself what she wanted to say.

'Go on, Leatherboots, out with it!'

'Well, here in the village, we have food, Pa has work, I'm not catching heads in a basket. Life is good, Salter.'

'Yes it is.'

'It's just that, do you ever, sometimes . . .'

'What?'

'. . . feel that something is missing?'

'Missin?' Salter's eyes widened. '*Missin.*' He rolled the word around his mouth. 'Well,' he said, 'since yer askin, I miss the old river.'

Moss sat up.

16

'Yes, I do,' said Salter. 'The rush and the roar of the big river. This little stream is nice and the fish are fat, but it ain't the Thames. Dirty and dangerous, that old river can snatch you quick as a rat's fart and roll yer body like a barrel. But on a good day it's wide and bright as the sea. And I think about the shack and the smoker and the sound of that old river breathin in and out on the shore. So if I was honest, and I don't see why I should be, but if I was, then I miss it.'

Salter eyes were shining as the memory of his old life poured from his lips. Now Moss thought about it, it made sense that he missed the river that he'd rowed and fished all his life. She wondered how often his thoughts drifted back to those old ways.

'So what about you, Leatherboots?'

'Me?'

'You said yerself, life is good here. So what's the problem?'

'It's kind-of hard to explain. All my life I dreamed of being far away from the Tower and the Hill and, you know, the *executions*. To be free. To be with Pa, living somewhere just like this, in a village with fields and bluebell woods.'

'So? Ain't too many that get their dreams fer real.'

'Yes, but now we're here,' Moss stared at the slow burn of the fire, logs shedding their feathery ash. 'Now we're here and everything's fine, well, I guess there's room to think of other things.'

'Such as?'

'Well, things . . . from our past. Do you ever think of your father and your mother?'

Salter blinked.

'I was just wondering,' she said.

Salter's gaze dropped. He shuffled the embers with the toe of his boot.

'Spend too long in the past,' he said, 'And you might not find yer way back.'

The fire spat. On his pallet, Pa shifted.

Salter stood up. 'I'm turnin in. Much as I'd like to, can't hang about all night chit-chattin.'

'Night, Salter.'

But he didn't reply. Moss watched him splash a little water on his face from the bucket. Then he disappeared into his corner, drawing the heavy wool curtain behind him.

CHAPTER THREE
The Promise

'Moss!' Pa was calling from the forge.

'Coming Pa!' Moss beat the soil from her hands and clomped in from the vegetable patch where she'd been digging up skirrets. Pa was already pumping the bellows, sparks shooting out of the fire.

'Here.' She shook the skinny fist of roots. 'Not too bad for a second crop. If Salter gets us some rabbits, we'll have a good stew.'

Salter had gone at first light. Moss had heard him from her pallet in the little alcove by the fire.

She'd said nothing, just listened to the sound of him pulling his boots on, munching on a hunk of bread while he dressed. She'd wriggled down under her blanket. These noises were as familiar to her now as the crackle of logs. It was as though Salter had always lived with them.

Pa was tying the beaten leather apron behind his back. She looked to the table. On it was a little jug with a sprig of hazel poking out of the top. She'd placed it there for Pa that morning before she'd gone out. All those months ago when she'd walked out of the Tower with no word of where she was going, Pa was so distraught it had almost killed him. A sprig of leaves or a few flowers left in the jug was her unspoken way of telling him that she was coming back. That she loved him.

'Farmer Bailey's bringing up Big Sal for shoeing this morning,' said Pa. 'She's an old mare and no mistake. Most wouldn't bother with an animal you can neither ride nor work. But Farmer Bailey's got a soft spot for that horse.'

'I've seen him,' said Moss. 'He leads her to the sweetest meadow grass. Talks to her while she eats.'

Pa smiled. 'Would you say she listens?'

'Yes, I'm sure she does. And you know, Pa, I think Big Sal talks to Farmer Bailey too.'

Pa nodded. 'It's a rare friendship, that one. Men like to think they are the master of beasts. But I don't think Big Sal would agree.' He took down the hammer, tongs and creaser from their hooks on the wall.

Moss watched him lay his tools neatly next to the anvil. Gentle, careful Pa. Who avoided the river if he could and liked to walk the woods at sunset. Moss had spent many evenings last autumn crunching through the leaves by his side. This way, little by little, Moss had learnt of her mother. That she was green-eyed and tangle-haired. That she had freckles on her nose and a dimple in her cheek and was so much like her daughter. That she sang when she was sad. That she'd once climbed to the top of a tree to pick a red-ripe apple, just for Pa.

Moss clutched at these fragments of her mother. But no matter how hard she tried to make Pa's memories her own, she couldn't. They were from a distant place that only he could reach. All the same, she clung to them. They were all she had.

'There are still blackberries in West Woods,' said Moss. 'I'll go up there now, see if I can catch Salter on his way back.'

'Just a minute.'

'What is it?'

'Over there,' said Pa. 'There's something for you.'

'For me?'

There was a sackcloth bundle on the table, tied with string.

'Open it,' said Pa.

Moss pulled at the string and the sackcloth fell away. Inside was more cloth, a smooth, tightly-woven wool. Carefully, Moss picked it up, unfurled it.

'Oh, Pa.'

It was a dress. Soft and green. The colour of new leaves.

'Pa, how did you –?'

'We've been plenty busy since we got here,' he said. 'Shod horses, mended hoes, made new knives for the innkeeper. Our first year was a good year, Moss. And you've outgrown those old rags you've had since goodness knows when.'

'But this must have cost so much, Pa.'

'Well, never mind that.' He smiled and his tired face brightened, and Moss could see how happy it made him to give her this dress.

'I'll try it on,' she said.

She tucked herself into her little alcove, pulled off her old dress and tugged the new one over her head. The wool was light against her skin. Compared to the scratch of the coarse garments she'd always worn, this was like stepping into silk. She stared down at herself, then felt suddenly shy.

'Well?' said Pa, 'Does it fit you?'

'It does, Pa,' said Moss, 'It's the most beautiful dress.'

She wrapped her skinny arms tight around him. Pa

had worked so hard to build this life for them. How could she possibly think something was missing?

'Pa,'

'Yes?'

'Do you sometimes think of her?'

Pa loosened Moss's hug so he could look into her face.

'Your mother?'

Moss nodded.

'Yes, I do.'

'Does she seem far away?'

'Well, yes and no. Sometimes I think I can still hear her.'

'Really?'

'Not actual words. It's more . . . the *feel* of her voice. Outside. In the grass, or blown by the wind.'

'And do you . . . do you ever, *see* her?'

Pa's gaze went through Moss, to that distant place only he could reach. 'Perhaps just a trace. It's been so long.' He smiled. 'Do you think your old Pa's a little crazy?'

'No, Pa.' She hugged him tight. 'I really don't.'

Outside, there was a clatter of hooves. A ruddy-cheeked man poked his head into the forge.

'Mornin, Samuel!'

'Morning, Farmer Bailey,' said Pa. 'Got Big Sal with you? Tie her to the post. I'll be right out.'

As Moss left the forge, Pa and Farmer Bailey were deep in talk of horses and Big Sal and how fine a friend she was to Farmer Bailey, who would be sorry to lose her when the time came.

Moss hopped over the fence and waded through the long meadow grass. Salter would be well into the woods by now, checking his traps. Thank goodness for rabbits, she thought, for there was precious little meat. Here in the village, the sheep were for wool or milk and the pigs went to market. She hadn't seen a ham since Twelfth Night. What a ham it had been, though. On Mrs Bailey's kitchen table, glistening with honey and pocked with cloves. And Mrs Bailey must have seen her face pop, because she'd sent a good piece round to Pa the next day. They'd eaten it that evening, savouring every morsel of that sweet, spiced meat. But mostly they lived on stew made from the vegetables that Moss grew, fish from the river and bread bought with Pa's earnings. And the rabbits.

It was poaching of course. The woods belonged to Sir John, and although Salter said the gamekeepers were as dozy as a cow in a hot field, he risked a chopped hand if he was caught. Nevertheless, he'd become bold and somehow he always seemed to be one step ahead. He lured the rabbits with cabbage leaves and turnips. He never set his traps in the same place. He was crafty and quiet. Neither the keepers nor the rabbits stood a chance.

By the treeline, Moss found the blackberry bushes and had just begun to fill her basket when she spotted Salter coming out of the woods with several grey rabbits flopped over his shoulder.

'Four young bucks,' said Salter. 'Not a bad mornin's work.'

'Enough for stew.'

'And some left over. Goin to take em to the Nut Tree now, see if I can't sell a couple to Old Samser.'

'I'll come with you.'

'If you like, but leave the barterin to me, Leatherboots, or I'll end up with nuppence for me trouble.'

'But I always feel so sorry for Old Samser. This isn't *London*, where everyone's looking for a way to rip each other off, you know. They do things differently here.'

'You reckon so? Well, don't feel too sorry for that old goat. He may be slow, but he ain't stupid. If I let him, he'd play me like a fiddle. Anyway, a bit of bargainin keeps everyone on their toes.'

It was only ten o'clock but already smoke was puffing from the windows of the Nut Tree Inn. Salter pushed at the door and they threaded their way through the tumble of voices. No one batted an eyelid at the rabbits. Like Salter, many of the villagers poached for a bit of meat and the Nut Tree was where you sold or traded any you couldn't eat yourself.

Old Samser stood at the top of the cellar steps, jug in hand. Wagging her tail against his leg was Poppy, Old Samser's spaniel, staring up at Salter's rabbits with hopeful eyes.

'Eyes off them rabbits, Poppy,' said Salter, letting the dog lick his hand. 'They ain't fer you.'

Old Samser chuckled. 'Mornin, Moss, mornin, Salter-boy. What you got there, then?'

'Two young bucks, Samser, if I likes the price.'

Moss knelt down beside Poppy and ruffled her shaggy coat, catching a wink from the old landlord. He was well used to Salter's cheekiness.

'Bain't no lad in the village can trap rabbits like the boy here. He's a sly city fox, this one. If he can't get yer one way, he'll get yer another.'

'A groat buys you two rabbits, take it or leave it,' said Salter.

'Threefarthin,' said Old Samser.

'Are you out of yer mind? Three pennies and I ain't goin no lower.'

'Two pennies and yer backsides can warm themselves by my fire.'

'Our backsides don't need warmin,' said Salter. 'No deal.'

Moss found herself smiling. She had to admit, there was something very satisfying about watching Salter hold his nerve. But Old Samser wasn't backing down just yet.

'Two pennies and a jug of my best to take back for yer Pa.'

Salter shook his head. 'You'll have to do better than that, landlord.'

'All right then, two pennies, three farthin and the jug.'

'Three pennies and you can have the pick of these fine rabbits, whichever two you like.'

Old Samser chuckled. 'All right, all right. Three pennies it is. It's a hard bargain you drives,

'And what of the new Queen?' asked Old Samser. 'We heard she is with child.'

'Yes, yes, there's much talk of Queen Jane. Grown fat as a pot-bellied oak and took to her chambers at Hampton Court some weeks back. The King has set a guard around the walls that would keep out the whole French army! Pray for all our sakes she gives him a son and heir.'

'Even a king needs the luck.' Old Samser twisted the end of his beard. 'We in these parts hopes the best for Queen Jane. Grew up not five mile from here, in Savernake.'

'Is that so?' said the drover. 'Well, she'll squeeze out her pup soon enough. If it's a boy, she may keep her title and her head. If not, then I wouldn't be in her dainty shoes for all the crowns in Christendom. Old Harry is going through wives like a pig through a bag of carrots!'

'True enough,' said Old Samser, and he began to chant, '*Queen Catherine left to rot poor soul, Queen Anne went for the chop.*' The rhyme produced a ripple of laughter from the drinkers.

Moss swallowed. She hated the songs and the jokes. People had never liked Anne Boleyn. When she was alive, they'd called her the Firecracker Queen. Now she was dead they called her a witch and had only cruel things to say in her memory. But Moss had met the Queen. Two winters ago in a snow-covered garden at Hampton Court. Hungry and cold, Moss had followed her nose through a kitchen window, eaten a pigeon and strayed into the Kings Garden. And when the Queen had found her there, instead of being angry and calling for the guards, Anne Boleyn had talked to her. She'd told Moss how the King had loved her once, how she'd made him laugh and how she'd gone looking for adventure. And though at the time she'd seemed full of mischief, when Moss thought of her now it was as a wandering ghost, frail and forlorn.

Moss's hand went to her pocket. In it was the little silver bird she always kept there. A gift from Queen Anne. Even though the silverwork was very fine, she'd never thought to sell it. It had saved her life. *Hold on to love, wherever you can find it,* the Queen had told her. *It is a most precious thing.* The words had settled, like leaves on a pond.

'What you waitin for Leatherboots? Come on!' Salter was on his feet and heading out of the door, coins jangling in his pocket.

She followed him outside, then stopped. 'You go on. I'll catch you up.'

Salter nodded. 'Two rabbits, three pennies. That's a good mornin's work.' He slung the rabbits over his shoulder. 'Oh, Leatherboots,'

'Yes?'

'Yer new dress. Looks, well . . . all right.'

Moss felt her cheeks flush and turned quickly in the other direction. She didn't think he'd noticed. And anyway, what did it matter if he had?

All Moss could hear was birdsong.

It was a quietness that she knew she would never

take for granted. No shouts, no rumble of cartwheels, and no one to call her back. The clamour of the city was a world away from the lush green fields that lay before her. Moss hitched up her dress and climbed the fence, dropping onto the grass on the other side. This was a well-worn shortcut to the place where she and Salter swam and fished, and she hurried there eagerly now.

The water was clear. Flowing gently once more. But the river felt different. On the banks the fish stranded yesterday had begun to rot, their scales curling to a dull grey.

Moss pulled out her apple-sack tunic from the willow tree. There was no one about, but she couldn't quite bring herself to change on the open riverbank, so she darted into the bushes. Still damp from yesterday, the cloth was cold against her skin.

Back on the riverbank, she stared out over the water. The crowfoot stroked the river bed, soothing her thoughts. Into her head shimmered the face she thought she'd seen, its green eyes so like her own.

Slowly Moss lowered herself from the bank into the water. As always, the cold took her breath away. She bobbed her shoulders under, panting short gasps until her body got used to the numbing chill. Then she kicked off from the bank and dived down. Halfway across she stopped and stood to watch the sway of the crowfoot. There was nothing here. Just waterweed.

Moss lay back in the current and then flipped over, sinking her head below the surface. She blinked as the water swirled past her eyes. The chalk river was so clear she could see all the way to the stones on the bottom. Moss had never stopped marvelling at this shimmering world. It was a quiet place that belonged to the creatures and plants, and Moss was always glad to be among them.

Something caught her eye. Hidden among the weeds. She could not make it out. A dark shape. A shadow. Moving away from her.

Moss kicked her feet hard, trying to reach the

crowfoot before the shadow disappeared. She parted the weed, following the tail of the shadow, feeling slippery greenness all around.

Where are you?

Could a ghost hear your thoughts?

She bobbed her head above the water to take another gulp of air and when she sank back down, there it was.

The face.

Green eyes, hair coiling, arms reaching. A gentle face, smooth as milk. A mirror of herself. And Moss could not help but stretch her own arms towards the ghostly figure.

She felt her hands clasped by ice-cold fingers.

Who are you?

The gentle ghost tried to smile, as though she had understood Moss's unspoken question.

But something was wrong.

The face was changing. The milk-smooth skin was flaking away. Peeling, tearing, paper-thin flakes hanging from her cheeks. The ghostly mouth parted as if to say something, then began dissolving before Moss's eyes. Now it gaped at Moss, half torn, teeth rooted in bare bone. A dead face. A skull face, lit by strange candle eyes. A face Moss knew too well.

The Riverwitch.

Moss wrenched her hands from the bone-cold grasp and burst to the surface. She scrabbled backwards, splashing and stumbling, trying to reach the bank. But winding its way round her ankles was the twisting waterweed, holding her fast to the river bed.

Up through the clear water rose the Riverwitch. Her tattered dress rippled outwards, her skull face breaking the surface of the river.

'River Daughter . . . now the Blacksmith's Daughter, are you not?'

'I . . . I thought you had gone,' said Moss.

The Riverwitch said nothing.

'Why?' asked Moss. 'Why have you come back?'

'You know why.' The Witch's eyes flared. 'I saved your life when you were born. But in return a promise was made. You were to come to me on your twelfth birthday.'

'And I did come. That day on the river. I jumped. I gave myself to you.'

Above the trickle of the river the Witch's voice hissed, 'Tell me, what do you remember of that day?'

Moss opened her mouth to speak. Some of it was so clear – stepping from the raft into the murky water where the Riverwitch lay waiting, Salter's cry as she was dragged down. But after that the pictures in her head ran thin as a poor man's broth. There was the darkness of the deep river. The bone-arms of the Riverwitch circling her. Moss's own arms embracing that cold body. And as she'd drifted into blackness, the grasp of the Witch had slackened. Then she remembered no more.

'Why?' said Moss. 'Why did you let me go?'

The Riverwitch inclined her head slowly. 'The embrace of a child.' She spread her arms. 'The embrace of a child has the power to thaw a Witch's frozen heart.'

'So . . .'

'So that day I let you go. But do not forget. You were promised to me. A child born in water, you shall return to water. You *belong* to me.'

'No!' Moss kicked out at the coils of weed that bound her feet, but they held fast.

'Do not struggle. You cannot fight me, River Daughter. I am the swirl and suck of the river. Its currents and its mysteries pass through me. They have made me strong. And I have watched you swimming the river. I've seen your eyes open to its treasures and its terrors.'

Something clicked inside Moss's head.

'The mud yesterday, in the river . . . It was sucking me down,' she said, 'but something pulled me free. Was it *you*?'

The Witch's face stretched into a painful smile.

'But why?' said Moss. 'Why save me again, if you are going to take me now?'

The water began to churn and the Witch grew suddenly agitated, her body twisting, the fronds of her dress whisking this way and that.

'There is something you can do for me,' said the Witch slowly, 'A way for you to earn your freedom.'

'My freedom?' echoed Moss.

'What I ask will not be easy. But if you succeed, I will release you.'

The churning river quietened and for a few moments there was just silence between them, the Witch's body swaying in the current.

'Isn't that what you want, River Daughter? Isn't that what you've always wanted?'

Moss hesitated. 'What is it?' she asked. 'This thing you want me to do?'

'All in good time, River Daughter. First you must leave this village.'

'Leave? Leave Pa and Salter?'

'Leave this place. Go back. To London.'

'But London is miles and miles. Three days walk at least.'

'You shall travel by river.'

'But I can't just disappear. Pa needs me.'

The Witch's lantern eyes held her. *How could I have mistaken this face for my mother's?* thought Moss. She'd wanted to believe it so badly. But all the time it was the Riverwitch.

The Witch held up two ghostly hands. The tips of her fingers were black. She gestured to the dead fish on the bank.

'It has begun,' she said.

'What has begun?'

But the Witch's torn body was sinking back into the river. As the weed closed over her head, her words mixed with the trickle of water.

'The river rots . . .'

Then Moss felt the tendrils loosen around her feet.

The Riverwitch had gone.

CHAPTER FOUR
Boat Thief

It was unthinkable.

Wasn't it?

Moss lay back on her pallet staring at the ceiling.

Even if she took Salter's boat, she'd never been further than a few miles down river. Salter had told her, though, that if you went far enough the gentle chalk river gathered speed until it met the wide path of the Thames. Flowing past fields and towns to London. There it became the murky torrent she knew, raging through the arches of London

Bridge and all the way out to the sea.

But why did the Witch want her to go there? What did she want from Moss?

She rolled over and kicked off her blanket. She couldn't *breathe* in here.

What if she didn't go? What if she stayed here? If she never went near a river again, the Witch couldn't touch her.

Freedom . . . isn't that what you've always wanted?

This past year and a half here in the village, with Pa and Salter, Moss had experienced more freedom than she'd ever dreamt was possible. And now she thought about it, the river was a huge part of her new life. Salter fished it, she swam in it. To run from the Riverwitch now would mean giving all that up.

Softly she slipped from her pallet and tweaked the curtain. The forge was heavy with Pa's deep sleep. No noise from Salter. In those early days, when Salter had let her stay in his cosy shack, Moss had discovered he was a light sleeper, always half an eye open in case of trouble. But since coming to live in the forge he'd slept like a boy who'd been turned to stone.

Moss pulled on her dress and boots. She patted her pocket. The little bird was there. Then she laid out her blanket. On it she placed a knife, a wooden mug, half a loaf of bread, some cheese and her tinderbox. Reaching under her pallet, she pulled out her winter shawl, given to her by Mrs Bailey last year when the frost came. If nothing else, she could sell it to buy food. Folding the blanket over these few possessions, she tied the ends together and slung it over her back.

Even in boots, her steps were soft on the earth floor. She knew Pa would not wake. There could be no goodbye of course, stealing away in the middle of the night. But at least she could let him know she was coming back. As quietly as she could, she opened a shutter and plucked a sprig of red-berried hawthorn from the bush that grew outside their window. Tiptoeing to the table, she removed the hazel from the jug and replaced it with the hawthorn. Then she tweaked the curtain to Pa's pallet and took a last look at her sleeping father.

The great bear-frame of his body rose and fell. A frown creased his face and Moss wondered where he went in his dreams. She was sorry that he'd wake up and find her gone. But Salter was there to help in the forge and pick the skirrets, and in any case, she hoped she would return soon enough.

Outside, the fields were pink-orange in the glow of the harvest moon. Moss heaved her bundle over the fence and clambered after it. The grass, damp with night dew, brushed her legs. She crossed the fields quickly and then she was at the river.

She didn't feel good about taking Salter's boat. He'd made it himself from pieces of old timber he'd found on the Baileys' farm. It lay upturned on the bank. She heaved it over, half-expecting it to cry out for its master, but the only sound was the slap of wood against water as she slid it into the river. She tethered it to a tree stump and threw her bundle in.

'Goin somewhere?'

'Oh!' Moss jerked round. 'What are *you* doing here?'

'I could ask you the same thing, Leatherboots. Sneakin off in the night. Takin me boat and whatever else you got in that bundle.'

'It's just food and a few things for the journey.'

'Journey, eh? Goin far?'

'Down the river.' There was no point lying. Though she didn't have to tell him the whole truth.

'Is that right? All by yerself? This river ain't no gentle row. You may be able to manage up here, but downriver it'll whip along fast and furious.'

'I know. You don't have to tell me.'

'Then what's this all about, shore girl? And why creep off in the night, not a word to me nor yer Pa?'

'You wouldn't understand.'

'Try me.'

'I don't even understand it myself. It's just a feeling.'

'Well I got a feelin. A *bad* feelin. You been funny ever since yesterday in the river. And whatever it is that you ain't tellin me, it's makin you do a stupid thing.'

'It's not stupid. And anyway, even if it was, you're not my keeper. I can do what I like, Salter. Go where I like.'

Salter considered this. 'All right then.' He threw his leather bag into the boat.

'What are you doing?'

'Comin with you.'

'You are not.'

'Try and stop me. Anyway, that's my boat yer in.'

'Fine. Suit yourself.'

She watched him push off from the bank and hop on board. They wobbled into the current. Moss took the oars and began to row. Salter sat back.

'Cheer up, Leatherboots! It'll be good to see that old city again.'

'Who said anything about London?'

'Call it a feelin.'

'Good or bad?'

Salter looked at Moss. She waited for the crinkle in his eyes, but none came.

'Too early to say,' he said.

CHAPTER FIVE
Bonfires and Cannons

There was something unreal about the day that followed. Ignored by the creatures that swam and nested and bobbed, Salter's boat was as quiet as the river and Moss was glad of the silence. When she wasn't rowing, she leant over the side, staring into the clear water.

She hadn't told Salter about the Riverwitch. Though he'd been there through it all and had seen the Witch for himself, once they'd left London, Salter had been as keen as Moss to start their new life and bury those memories deep. He'd never wanted to talk about it. And Moss, who'd never really forgiven herself for putting her friend in such terrible danger, had vowed never to risk Salter's life again. Despite his stubbornness, following her and jumping into the boat, she would do everything in her power to keep him away from the Riverwitch.

That evening they struck camp well before dusk, dragging the boat into a field. Moss gathered stout branches to prop underneath the upturned boat. It would be good shelter that night from the cold and rain. Grudgingly she accepted Salter's offer to fish for their supper. It turned out he'd brought many things in his bag. His hooks and line, a hatchet, a pan to cook with and even some onions from her storebox. And before she knew it, they began to fall into familiar ways. Moss gathered wood and by the time Salter had a fish wriggling on the end of his line, the fire was lit and the pan was hot. That night they slept curled under the boat in their blankets.

When the birds woke them at daybreak, Moss insisted they pack up and move on straight away. They launched the boat back on to the river and Salter took the oars, while Moss settled back in her place at the front. Though she never took her eyes from the water, she saw nothing but riverweed and trout.

Before long the river grew wider. If there were coots or moorhens on this stretch, they didn't show themselves. Once or twice Moss saw places where the grassy banks seemed to shrink from the water's edge, pushed back by an oozing sludge. She caught glimpses of dead fish, slits of tarnished silver in the mud. And there was a smell. A rotten smell. Of dead things and fly-blown meat. A smell that had no place in a fresh, cold river.

They rowed all day, taking turns, sharing half a loaf of bread and some cheese, until their boat was gathered by the tug of the big river Thames as it swept past villages and towns towards London.

'Can't be more than twenty miles from the

city now.' Salter was rowing. It was almost sunset. 'We'll have to moor up somewhere soon.'

Moss dragged her gaze from the river and began looking up and down the banks for a good place to land. Through the branches of the tall oaks, she caught a flash of something bright. She stood up, craning her neck to get a better view.

'Oi! Sit down!'

This broad sweep of river, it was familiar.

'Just a minute. I think I know where we are.'

Lit by the October sun, a golden-turreted gatehouse rose above the trees.

'Roll me in a barrel and drown me now!' said Salter. 'Ain't that a sight.'

He steered the little boat round the wide river bend and there, spreading either side of the five-storey gatehouse, were the elegant brick walls of Hampton Court Palace.

'Well, you can see why the King brings all his ladies down here. *That* is one fancy pile of bricks.' Salter drew in the oars and let the boat glide with the current. 'Ain't this the place you told me you snuck into? Thieved a pigeon and a cloak if I remember right?'

'I was desperate.'

'Just like I always said. You learnt good that night, Little Miss Stealin-Ain't-Right. Bread first, then morals.'

Moss rolled her eyes. It was true though. She'd never forget that feeling. So hungry, she'd have done almost anything to get her hands on some food. A different time. A frozen river. The palace covered in snow. She gazed at the high walls. How on earth had she managed it? She'd clambered through a kitchen window. There'd been hardly a guard in sight. Not like today. She stared at the line of armoured soldiers, pikestaffs pointing to the sky. The drover was right. King Henry was guarding his new queen as though she was made of glass.

As they drifted nearer, they could see there was quite a crowd gathered in front of the gatehouse. Moss could hear chatter and the cries of hawkers. The smell of spices and roast meat wafted on to the river.

'Now *that's* what I'm dreamin of, night in, night out.' Salter licked his lips. 'Warm gingerbread an' mutton with the fat drippin down me chin.'

He dipped the oars back into the river, slowing the boat. 'Why don't we stop here? Just for a bit?' He patted his pocket. 'Got me three pennies. I'll buy you a pie.'

'Well,' said Moss, 'so long as we pay for it fair and square.'

'What do you take me for?' said Salter, grinning. 'I'm an honest country boy now! All me rough edges hacked off good an' proper.'

Somehow Moss doubted that was quite true, but she was hungry. And this was as good a place as any to try and find a field for the night.

Salter was hauling at the oars, but before he could turn the little boat towards the bank, a whip of current spun them around.

'Whoah!' he cried. 'What was that?'

'What?'

'Get off!'

'What's the problem?'

Salter was tugging at his left oar.

'Somethin . . . somethin's got me paddle!'

Moss crawled to the middle of the boat and grabbed the oar. She could feel it. Something was pulling from below.

Splash! The oar flew from their grasp and landed in the water.

'Quick!' Salter leant over the side, trying to rake the floating oar back towards the boat.

All around them the grey water was turning green.

'Salter –'

Thick coils of snaking waterweed were circling the boat.

'Salter, forget the oar –'

'Hell's Chickens! Where did all this weed come from?'

'Salter! Forget the oar! Hold on!'

'What?' For a split second, he looked up at

Moss and saw her shocked face. Then they both grabbed the sides of the boat.

It all happened so fast. The boat flipped over, slamming the pair of them into the river. Moss felt her back ram against the upturned seat. Twisting round, she grabbed the boat and held on as best she could, but it surged forward with a force strong enough to carve its way through boulders. Her eyes were blind in the rush of water. All she could hear was the roar of the river. She spluttered and shouted, but could not move, pinned as she was, arms wrapped round the seat, clinging and gasping, feeling her grip slackening and knowing that if she let go, she'd be snatched by the current and tumbled in its fists like a rag in a boilpot.

All at once, she felt a great weight bearing down on the top of the upturned boat. The water choked her throat. She spluttered and retched, then something knocked the wind from her chest and the tumbling water faded away.

Boom! Boom! BOOM!

Such a pounding her ears had never felt. A storm ripping through her head. Thunder and lightning exploding all around her, loud enough to burst her eyes from their sockets.

In her mouth, the taste of mud. Her cheek against something wet and slippery, her eyes gummed shut and her body battered. She rubbed the mud from her eyes and lifted her head. She was lying on shingle, the river lapping her feet. The air was clogged with smoke. The boat was nowhere to be seen. Just a few feet away lay Salter. On his back, mouth open, eyes closed.

Moss crawled towards him, her knees scraping on the stones. She reached out and touched his hand. It was cold. She pressed her ear to his chest, but against the pounding explosions in the night sky, she could hear nothing.

'Salter . . .' She rolled his body on to its side. It convulsed and she watched as he erupted in a fit of coughing. Salter opened his eyes and they widened at the deafening noise all around them.

'Devil eat me breeches,' he croaked, 'What the hell is goin on?' He was looking about, but they couldn't see a thing. He sniffed the air.

'I'd know that smell anywhere,' he said.

'What smell?' All Moss could smell was smoke.

'Salt-mud. Smell of the old river.'

'What? Are you crazy?' But as she spoke, a sudden wind blew the smoke away and she staggered to her feet, almost toppling backwards into the mud.

Rising like a cliff in front of her were the sheer and mighty walls of the Tower of London.

She could not speak. Her head throbbed and she swayed, staring with disbelief from the Tower to the river to Salter and back to the Tower.

Now she could see that the deafening explosions were coming from inside the Tower itself. Cannons. Volley after volley. And all along the river, bonfires were burning. Had they woken up in some great battle? Washed up on the shore, only to be trampled by the stamping horses of an invading army?

Then the cannons stopped. The last wisps of smoke drifted away and in their place came the sound of cheering and laughter.

'Somethin's goin on,' Salter pulled her arm. 'Come on, let's get near one of them fires, dry ourselves out.'

Moss hitched the skirts of her waterlogged dress and followed Salter up the bank to where an enormous bonfire blazed, flames snapping at the night sky.

A crowd was gathered around the fire. Two men in velvet caps filled mugs from a barrel as fat as a pony.

'Bring your mugs and your jugs!' cried one of the men. 'Fill them up and drink them down and be as merry as you please, this night of nights!'

'City merchants givin out free beer?' said Salter. 'Has the world gone mad?' He marched up to the men.

'Beer for you, lad?' said the red-cheeked merchant.

'What's the night, mister?'

The merchant seemed taken aback by Salter's question. 'Where've you been this day, lad? Snoring under a hay bale?'

'It's a long story,' said Salter.

The merchant laughed and raised his mug. 'The Queen has had her child. The King has a son! Long live the Prince! We toast his health and thank heaven and all the angels, for England's throne has an heir at last!'

There was a huge cheer from the men and women around the bonfire. Mugs clanked and the merchants' boys threw on more logs. Now the smoke had cleared, Moss could see that London Bridge was a blaze of torches. Men dangled from the arches waving their arms. Long flags fluttered from the rooftops and the whooping carried down the river. It seemed to her as if all London had come out to shout and sing for the new prince.

'Come on,' said Salter. 'We need to look for the boat and our stuff before the tide takes it back.'

Moss looked at the black river doubtfully. But

she knew he was right. If there was a chance they could find it, they had to try. A broken boat and two wet blankets were better than nothing at all.

They scrambled back to the water's edge and worked their way up the shoreline, prodding and scouring. But all they found were bits of old crate, bricks and bones, coughed up by the tide.

'This is hopeless.' Moss turned from the river and stared up the shore. Not far off, slumped like a tired army in the mud, were the fishermen's tumbledown huts.

Salter was shaking his head. 'Where *is* it?' he muttered.

'Let's face it, the boat's gone,' said Moss. 'We need to find somewhere to sleep. *Salter?*'

'Here,' he said. 'It was *here*.' He was dashing to and fro like a mouse that had lost its hole. 'It was *here*. I swear on me old nan's teeth.'

Then he stopped. Sniffed the air. And looked down. Now he was on his knees, scrabbling in the shingle.

'Salter, what are you doing?'

He pulled a piece of charred wood from the stones. 'The smoker . . .' He took a few steps forward and blinked with disbelief, turning in a slow circle and looking at the ground. He was standing on what could only be described as a pile of broken sticks.

And then she understood.

'Oh, Salter, I'm sorry –'

'Me old shack. It's gone.'

Moss stared helplessly at where Salter's hut had been. Never much to look at from the outside, inside the shack had been snug as two cats. Now it was smashed to tinder. A heap of wood, barely enough for an hour's blaze.

'Salter,' she said gently, 'it can't be helped. All those children on the riverbank, hungry and frozen. When they realised you weren't coming back, they'd have taken what they could. Come on. You'd have done the same.'

'Maybe I would,' said Salter gruffly. 'But you ain't never built somethin with yer bare hands, only to find it pulled to pieces like a chicken from its bones . . . Wait a minute.' He patted his pockets. 'Cussin collops!' He kicked at the ground, sending a spray of shingle into the river. 'All me coins must've fallen out.'

No money, no blankets and no boat. At least there were fires on the shore. There was a chance they wouldn't freeze to death. They traipsed back to the bonfire and sat huddled together, backs to the heat, as close as they could get without setting themselves alight. And Moss must have forgotten the cold, because at some point she felt her head fall gently against Salter's shoulder.

In the distance, cries and cheers mixed with the hush of the waves.

'You asleep, Leatherboots?' murmured Salter.

She was too tired to reply. But as sleep came, she felt the lightest touch of something soft on her forehead.

CHAPTER SIX
Cat's Head

A howling river wind woke Moss early next morning. She lifted her head and sat up. Salter was still asleep, propped against an empty beer barrel. She guessed he'd dragged it over to the fire to shield them from the wind. She stood up and shook out her dress. It was smoky and specked with ash, but the wool was bone-dry next to her skin. Silently she thanked Pa. Without a blanket or a groat to her name, this dress was all she'd got.

'Arrggh.' Salter groaned himself awake. He

stretched and his neck cricked. 'Sweet Harry's achin bones! Feels like someone chopped me head off and put it back the wrong way.'

Moss didn't hear him. She was already down by the water's edge, walking along the shore. The strangeness of their river journey was fresh in her mind – snatched by a freak current and dumped right in front of the Tower.

'Hey! Leatherboots! Wait for me!'

Salter caught her up. 'Where are you goin?'

'Back to where we pitched up last night.'

'Won't do no good. Tide'll have taken the boat. Won't be nothin to find now.'

'I know. I just –' She broke off. What could she say? She wasn't going to tell him about the Riverwitch.

But Salter was distracted by something else. The grey river raked the shingle, leaving a sticky sludge in its wake.

'Steer clear of that mud, Leatherboots,' said Salter. 'You never know how deep this stuff is.

Maybe it's just an inch or two, or maybe it's sinkin mud.'

'Sinking mud?'

'Deep as a pit, thick as porridge – mud that'll trap you an' pull at yer boots an' the more you struggle, the more stuck you get. Till you ain't got the strength to even call out fer help. And when it knows you ain't goin nowhere, that mud will suck you down. Cold an' thick an' pressin the life from yer lungs. An' there ain't a thing you can do but watch yerself get swallowed slow.'

Moss stopped walking. 'That's what it felt like. That day the fish jumped out and I got stuck.'

Salter nodded. 'It's evil stuff an' no mistake, an' you don't go near it if you can help it.'

They were almost at Tower Wharf. A putrid smell crept past Moss's nostrils.

'Holy dogbits!' Salter's nose caught the wind. 'That's disgustin! I think I'm gonna gip.'

The closer they got to the Tower, the stronger the smell, until Moss's eyes were watering.

'Hold it, Leatherboots. *What* is *that?*'

Salter was pointing at a messy object, half buried in the mud not five feet from where they walked.

'Wouldn't touch it if I was –'

Too late. Moss was crouching by the muddy object, trying not to retch on the foulness that clawed its way down her throat.

It was a ball of matted fur, caked with river mud and what looked like old blood. Moss grabbed a stick and poked at it, rolling it over slowly. The matted fur was odd-looking. Speckled with a strange pattern, though it wasn't easy to see through all the mud. The ball tipped on its side.

'Oh!'

Moss jumped back.

Two startled eyes stared up at her – huge and black-ringed, faded by death. A lolling tongue poked through four enormous fangs. It was the head of some poor dead animal. Washed up by the tide.

Salter was beside her now. He whistled. '*That* is

one big cat. What's it been feedin on? All the other cats in town?'

'That's no cat,' said Moss.

'Got cat ears,' said Salter. 'Got cat eyes. And I reckon them straw things plastered to its fur are whiskers.'

'Look at its teeth,' said Moss. 'When did you last see a cat with fangs the size of parsnips?'

'Well, what is it then?'

'I don't know.'

'Hey, what are you doin? Don't touch that thing!'

Moss had lifted the head by the scruff of fur between its ears and was carrying it to the water's edge. It was heavy. She swilled it in the grey water until the mud had rinsed off. Then she carried it back up the shingle and laid it down.

The creature's head was covered in a strange pattern of round black patches, like a beautiful plague that spread from the line between its eyes across fawn-yellow fur.

'It's a good thing it's dead,' said Salter. 'Those

jaws would rip yer face off soon as look at you. Whatever that creature is, it ain't from round here.'

At Salter's words, something clicked inside Moss's head and it filled with the memory of animal roars from long ago.

'But it *could* be from round here.'

'Eh?'

'This creature. It could have come from the Tower.'

'*What?*'

'From the Beast House.'

Salter nodded slowly. "I heard about that place. Wolves an' snakes an' weird birds, ain't it?'

'I only know what the Tower folk told me. That they are the King's beasts. Rare and strange animals sent by the kings and queens of far away places.

'You ever see em?'

'No. I never went into the Beast House. Normal Tower folk weren't allowed, only the keepers. On Execution days we'd walk right past and I'd hear the animals howling and roaring, but the keepers kept it locked.'

'So,' said Salter, 'if you ain't never seen em, what makes you think that mangy head is one of em? An' even if it was, what's it doin washed up on the shore?'

'I don't know.'

She stared up at the Tower. Its walls gave nothing away. Once these walls had encircled her whole world. Where she and Pa had lived almost her entire life. Stark and sheer, they blocked the sky. A howl echoed across the turrets, joined by another and another, as if the animals of the Beast House were crying out, trying to reach beyond the walls. Moss had never heard them howl like that in all the time she had lived in the Tower.

She looked down at the head of the beast. Its face was a frozen snarl. However this creature had died, she was pretty sure it hadn't passed away peacefully in its sleep.

'We'll bury it,' she said.

'You what?'

'It shouldn't be here. We can't leave it slopping in and out with the tide.'

Salter spent the next ten minutes grumbling while they scrabbled a hole in the shingle near the bank, deep enough to take the creature.

When the head was buried, Moss walked back to the mudline.

The rotten smell was still there. It was everywhere. In her hair, in her nose. She could taste it on her tongue. It was the smell of death and it hung around the Tower like a stinking fog.

'Ready fer breakfast?'

'Not really. Anyway, we've no food. Or money.'

There was a flicker in Salter's eye. Tiny. But Moss caught it.

'Salter, no.'

'What?' He laughed. 'You don't even know what I'm plannin!'

'And I don't *want* to know.'

'Look, I ain't lyin to you. It's a scam all right. But it only takes from the pockets of them that can afford a groat or two. Nothin big. Nothin fancy. We won't get caught. All you need to do is –'

'*No*. Just . . . no. We've been in London one night and already you're talking about *thieving*?'

'You got a better idea? Unless you want to turn round an' walk back to the village right now?'

She didn't.

Right now they needed food and a place to sleep. Surely there must be someone who'd give them shelter. Just for a night or two.

'You lived on the river long enough,' said Moss, 'You *must* know somewhere we can go?'

'Ain't no one I can ask,' said Salter. 'It's every man, woman and child fer themselves in this city. Ain't no one who'll take us in without a groat to show fer ourselves.'

'Wait a minute,' said Moss. In her memory, a thought stirred. A name from the past. She'd never met him, but Salter had talked about him. A boy. Someone Salter went to for . . . well, she wasn't quite sure what he went to him for. But she remembered that he had helped Salter once, maybe twice.

'Eel-Eye Jack!' she cried. *That* was his name.

Salter's brow creased.

'Eel-Eye Jack,' said Moss.

'I heard you the first time. What about him?'

'He's your friend, isn't he?'

'Eel-Eye Jack ain't no friend.'

'You know what I mean. He helped you didn't he? Helped you find me when I went to Hampton that winter.'

'Eel-Eye Jack don't *help* people.'

'Oh, come on, Salter. We can ask him for a bed and a bit of food, just enough for a few days.'

'No.'

'What do you mean no?'

'I mean *no pussin way*. I mean Eel-Eye Jack ain't the kind to be askin favours from.'

'Salter, don't be ridiculous. We'll find a way to pay him back.'

'I'm serious. I ain't never been in debt to Eel Eye Jack. Done all me business on an equal foot. An' there's good reason for that. When he calls in his favours, you don't know what he'll ask.'

'What are you afraid of, Salter?' Moss could feel the heat rising in her throat. 'You don't want to ask for help? Is that it? You take care of yourself, let others take care of themselves. You'd lie and steal rather than ask a friend for help.'

'That's not true.'

'So prove it.'

Silence. She was up close to Salter. Close enough to see the trouble in the brown eyes that were gazing straight into hers.

She blinked. They both stepped back.

Salter kicked the shingle. 'All *right*. Have it your way. Just remember, he ain't my friend. An' whatever you think, he won't be no friend to you neither.'

CHAPTER SEVEN
Eel-Eye Jack

It was a long, winding walk from the river. Through shadows and alleys and back streets that twisted like the roots of a tree. Once or twice the two of them broke out into a wide street of painted shops and stalls, where they were squashed by the tide of people as they tried to cross. But Salter pulled Moss behind him and soon they were back in the dark lanes that squelched with the muck of horses and the spatterings of pisspots.

'Keep yer head up,' said Salter. 'Look like you

know where yer goin. Look like you ain't got a care in the world.'

Moss did her best, but she felt like a lamb lost in a forest. Watching her from the shadows were sly pairs of eyes. In fact, the further they went, the quieter the streets and the more convinced she became that they were being followed.

'Where is everyone?' she whispered. 'And why do I feel like we're not alone?'

'We've had scouts on us from Cheapside onwards. Eel-Eye Jack knows I'm comin.'

'Really?'

'We're on his patch now.' Salter stopped and faced Moss. 'Listen, Leatherboots. When we get there, let me do the talkin.'

'Why?'

'Because I know what he's like. I know how he works. An' I won't tell him any more than I have to.'

Moss shrugged. She didn't see what she could possibly talk about anyway. Lost in her own thoughts, she was happy to follow Salter, to let him do the talking, so long as they could get a place to sleep and a little food.

They were walking down another twisted alley. This one was so crowded with leaning roofs and tumbledown houses that daylight had given up on it entirely. Through the gloom, Moss could hear music. A fiddle, playing fast and furious. And as they rounded the corner, suddenly there was light. Squares of flickering gold, spilling from the windows of a building at the end. It was tall, many-floored and bent in all directions like a crooked hat.

Now the alley seemed full of the sawing fiddle and Moss heard shouts and the stamping of feet. Salter led her towards the bright building and stopped at the door. Hanging above it was a painted sign, rusted to an iron bracket. On it, a one-legged crow perched on a piece of mangled wood.

'Not a pretty sight, eh?' said Salter. 'But people don't come here fer pretty.'

Moss stared up at the sign. Beaten and faded, the

crow peered down at her and she wondered how it had lost its leg.

'Welcome to The Crow and Stump,' said Salter. 'You still sure this is what you want?'

Moss nodded.

'All right then. Stay behind me an' keep quiet.'

He pushed the door open and they walked in.

The fog of smoke inside was intense, but when Moss's eyes had stopped smarting she found herself in a large, rowdy inn. A topsy-turvy room of tables and jutting wooden platforms with steps and railings and ladders. Crammed into every corner were men clanking beer mugs, women who laughed and clapped to the music, and raggedy children dangling from the railings.

Filling the room with wild music was a boy. Older than Moss. Maybe fourteen or fifteen. He stood with his legs planted firm on the floorboards, holding a large fiddle to his chin. His bow was lightning quick, and the notes were clear and strong and soared up and around the room like swallows in the sky.

The boy seemed lost in his music, but as they threaded their way through people and tables, Moss saw that the boy's eyes were fixed on Salter, following as they crossed the room. And once they'd seated themselves on a step in the corner, his gaze kept flicking back to them and to Moss in particular. It was a curious gaze, thought Moss, but beyond that, she could not read it.

The music changed. Now the boy's strokes were deep and slow, and the inn filled with a sad, beautiful melody that settled inside Moss, drawing out memories of things long past, floating them into her head where they swirled with the music. All around her, the people of the inn nodded their heads, lifted from the room by their own rememberings. As Moss drifted with the melody, she became aware that the boy's blue eyes were now fixed on her. All this time Salter sat next to her, shifting on the step, as though impatient for the music to stop.

'What's the matter?' whispered Moss. 'It's beautiful. Don't you like it?'

'It ain't the music that bothers me. It's the one that's playin it.'

As Salter spoke, the boy finished playing, tucked the fiddle under his arm and strolled over to where they sat. He leant casually against the wooden rail of the stairs and tipped his head at Salter.

'Hello, Salter.'

'Eel-Eye.'

'It's been a long time. I heard you had left the city.'

'That's right.'

'I heard you were living in the fields with apple trees all around. Catching the stoats and milking the cows.'

There was something different about the way this boy spoke. As though he held something in the back of his throat. And there was a sing-song rhythm to his speech.

'So,' the boy went on, 'is it true? Are you a country boy now?'

'Maybe. It ain't such a bad life. You should try it yerself.'

'Maybe I will. Maybe I will come and visit you sometime, pick an apple from your tree.'

Moss watched this exchange. Two foxes circling each other. Voices smooth, hackles up.

Eel-Eye Jack turned to Moss. 'And you must be . . .?'

'Moss,' said Moss. 'I'm Salter's friend.' She felt a sharp dig in her ribs.

'Ahhh,' said Eel-Eye Jack. '*Friends . . .*' He drew up a chair and sat on it back-to-front, legs astride the seat, turning his full attention to Moss. 'And I always thought Salter was, how would you say, a lone wolf?' He swept his hand through the sand-blond hair that hung in sleek strands to his neck. 'Where are you from, Moss?'

'From –' Moss felt another jab in her side. 'From the village.'

Eel-Eye Jack laughed. 'Well, Moss-from-the-village, you are welcome in The Crow. We see the same old faces here and a new one is fresh air to blow away our dirty smoke.' He looked directly at

82

Moss as he spoke, his blue eyes bright, holding hers, as a flame would hold a moth.

Moss felt the words drop from her head. She didn't know what to say to this boy with his blue-flame eyes and sing-song words.

'I . . . I liked your music.'

Eel-Eye Jack took his fiddle from under his arm, sat on the step next to Moss and laid it across his knees. It was polished, walnut brown, etched with a twisting pattern of thorns.

'This fiddle has travelled far,' he said. 'From the cold countries across the sea.'

'The cold countries,' echoed Moss. 'Is that where you're from?'

Eel-Eye Jack smiled. 'In the cold countries they say that a good player has been taught by the devil himself. And in return, he gives a piece of his soul.'

'Oh . . . And what do you say?' said Moss.

Eel-Eye Jack leaned close to Moss and whispered in her ear. 'I say that maybe it is a bargain well struck.'

He pulled back and laughed and his eyes sparked mischief, as Salter's sometimes did. Moss couldn't help herself. She laughed too.

'All right, very funny I'm sure,' said Salter. He wasn't laughing and Moss sensed the irritation in his voice.

Eel-Eye Jack stood up. 'So what brings you to The Crow, Salter, my old friend? Can I call you that?'

'Call me what you like,' said Salter gruffly. 'We came to ask fer somethin.'

'Yes?'

'Food an' lodgins. One, maybe two nights.'

'You have money?'

Salter shook his head.

'Your boat?'

'Nope.'

'Then what are you bargaining with?'

'I ain't. I'm askin fer a favour.'

'A *favour* . . .' said Eel-Eye Jack, rolling the word on his tongue. 'A favour is not a thing I ever thought to hear you ask for.'

'Yeah? Well, I ain't askin twice.'

Eel-Eye Jack looked from Salter to Moss. 'For a favour,' he said, 'you can stay.'

'Fine,' muttered Salter.

'Thank you,' said Moss brightly. The music had lifted her heart and right now she couldn't think of a better place to stay than this warm, friendly inn.

After a word with the landlord, Eel-Eye Jack brought over a plate of bread and mutton. Moss and Salter ate ravenously and by the time they'd finished, they'd been given blankets too. They tucked themselves into a corner and Moss peeked out at the emptying tavern. The last thing she remembered was Eel-Eye Jack, leaning back against a staircase, eyes closed, the sad melody from his fiddle floating upwards with the smoke.

CHAPTER EIGHT
The Great White Bear

'Stone the crows an' the sparrers! That ain't worth no favour that I can think of.'

Salter and Moss sat at a table. In front of them were two bowls of grey porridge.

'Take it or leave it,' sniffed the landlord, 'That's all you're gettin unless Eel-Eye coughs up some more.'

They watched him shuffle back over to his barrels. They weren't the only ones who'd stayed the night in The Crow and Stump. Men and women lay

86

slumped in their chairs and on the rickety staircase a handful of children were curled up fast asleep. A fug of beer and smoke hung in the air. Of Eel-Eye Jack there was no sign.

Moss dug into her porridge, remembering the beautiful music of the night before. 'Eel-Eye Jack must have got up early,' she said. 'I'd like to hear him play again. I wonder when he'll be coming back?'

Salter eyed her. 'Better not ask too many questions about Eel-Eye,' he said. 'Wherever he is, it's *his* business and whatever that business is, you can bet yer guts it's dodgy.' He scraped the last of the porridge from his bowl. 'So . . . what you got planned fer our stay in the big city, Leatherboots?'

The question took Moss a little by surprise. In all the excitement of their arrival, she'd almost forgotten the Riverwitch.

'Well, I'm going to . . . just walk about a bit.'

'*Walk about a bit?* You came all this way to go fer a walk?' Salter laughed. 'Suit yerself. I'll come with you.'

Moss opened her mouth to object, but Salter was already on his feet.

'Fine,' she said. Hopefully he'd get bored and wander off by himself.

She wasn't sure how or where the Riverwitch would show herself, but one thing was certain, it wouldn't be here in The Crow and Stump. She needed to be down by the river.

They were standing next to Tower Wharf with the incoming tide slapping at their ankles.

'Crikey, Leatherboots, what are we doin back here? I didn't think you'd want to be within a pigeon's fart of the Tower.'

The truth was, Moss didn't know. It had seemed as good a place to start as any. She was fairly sure the freak current that had dragged them all the way to London had been the Riverwitch's doing. And they'd been dumped right in front of the Tower. That was no coincidence. She scoured the murk-dark water. There was no sign of the Witch.

'Ain't this where that old tunnel of yours is?' Salter was sloshing under the wharf.

'Wait!' Moss splashed after him. She'd almost forgotten about the tunnel. Rather, she'd *tried* to forget. Although it had been her escape route from the Tower, at high tide it flooded and last time she'd crawled in there she'd almost drowned.

'There you go,' said Salter, running his hand over the vague trace of a hole. The stones that blocked it were barely visible, hidden under a thick layer of oozing mud.

Moss stuck her hand in and tugged at one of the stones. 'Help me, will you?'

They pushed and pulled and eventually worked the stone loose enough to heave out. It splashed into the water and a thick brown sludge leached out after it.

'Ugh! Devil bite me nose off! That stuff stinks!' Salter staggered back.

Moss stared at the hole. The sludge moved slowly,

seeping from the gap where the stone had fallen. The whole tunnel was blocked. Floor to ceiling, choked with oozing, reeking mud.

'Ain't nobody going to be comin and goin through there no more then,' said Salter.

'I guess not.'

'Never liked it. Filthy crawlin rat-burrow of a place.'

They waded out from under the wharf and walked up the shore a little way, leaving the foul reek behind them. The shingle was dry and they sat together, halfway up the bank, staring out at the river.

It was the strangest feeling to be back, thought Moss. She'd wondered whether much would have changed in the year and a half she'd been away. She remembered how the river used to look from the Tower walls. On a sunny day she'd gaze down and it would sparkle up at her, silver-grey. Today, although the sun shone, the river was mud-brown. Still, it was packed. Barges nudged for a place on a quay, painted galleys unfurled their sails and the watermen steered their flat little boats, cussing their heads off as they rowed passengers from bank to bank.

Salter stretched and breathed in deep, filling his lungs. 'Salt river. Best smell in the world, ain't it? Don't tell me you haven't missed this, Leatherboots?' he said.

Moss smiled. 'I don't know if I've missed it exactly,' she said.

'No?' He closed his eyes and breathed in some more. 'Sprats, cockles, that's what I can smell. An' the tug of the current on me little boat.'

Moss closed her eyes too, remembering the first time she'd set foot on the shore. She could hear the swish of the waves rolling up and down the shingle, the noise of the river from inside Salter's shack. She loved that sound. It was the river breathing. In and out. Salter was right. She *had* missed it.

'I'm gonna take a walk up to Belinsgate. See the catch comin in,' said Salter. 'You comin?'

Moss shook her head. 'No, I'll stay here a bit. Follow you up there later.'

'Well don't be too long. I'll wait for you by the herring boats.'

'All right.'

She watched Salter pick his way up the narrow line of shingle until he was just a brown speck.

Now what? Surely the Riverwitch would show herself soon?

The wind was getting up, whipping a scum from the tip of the waves. In the distance among the bobbing boats, a barge was making its way up the river. Snatched by the wind and blown towards her, she could hear shouts from the deck along with a sound she'd not heard on the river before. An odd, strangled roar. She squinted, curious to see what was on that boat. She counted twelve men rowing and, as the boat got closer, the rowers began turning it to put in at Tower Wharf. She could see deckhands scurrying to and fro at the front. And as the barge turned, there was the strangest sight. A great beast, tethered to the deck. Moss had never seen anything like it. It looked like a bear. Yet unlike any dancing bear she'd ever set eyes on. Even on all fours it towered above the men. Its fur was creamy white. As she gaped at the bear, it threw its head back and another agonised roar spluttered from its jaws. Around its neck was an iron collar, welded to a chain that was stretched taut to a wooden post. Straining at each leg was a piece of thick rope, tied to four more posts. The bear tossed its head, trying to bite the chain from its neck, and the blood that leaked from its jaw had stained its muzzle red.

What was it doing here, this huge white bear? It was like a creature from a wild dream, thought Moss, from a faraway land of giants who hunted bears as tall as trees.

'Keep them ropes tight!'

'Watch out for its claws!'

'Don't let it come down too quick!'

The deckhands were shouting, throwing mooring ropes at the wharf. When the barge had been secured, they laid across a hefty gangplank. Moss watched as they untethered the great bear.

Surely it will pull free now, thought Moss. But from the wharfside came men with iron rods, the ends glowing as if they'd been heated in a fire. One of the men jabbed his rod at the bear and it flinched, grunting at sudden red-hot pain. The bear bowed its head and was led from the barge to the wharf, where two dozen men were ready to pick up the ropes. They hauled and prodded, and the beast lumbered to the steep path of Tower Hill. Were they taking it to the Tower?

A small crowd was buzzing now and Moss ran with them, up the hill. There were screams and cries of disbelief as the enormous bear shambled past them. All the while, the men with hot iron rods poked and jabbed, and each time it raised its head, Moss heard a low anguished growl and smelt singed fur. The portcullis cranked open and Moss's last view of the bear was of two powerful hind legs, trunks of thick white fur, disappearing through the arch of the Lion Tower.

By the time Moss and Salter returned to the alley, the open shutters of The Crow were coughing smoke into the twilight.

Inside, Eel-Eye Jack was seated at a corner table. His fiddle was by his side. A man was sitting opposite with his back to Moss and Salter, the blunt frame of his shoulders blocking the firelight. Moss noticed that the rest of the tavern was giving this table a wide berth. Only the landlord approached with a flagon of ale and, when the blunt man rose to leave, he scuttled back to his barrels on the other side of the inn instead.

When the man had gone, Eel-Eye Jack picked up his fiddle. He didn't seem in the mood for a foot-stomping tune, and sure enough the tavern soon echoed with a melody that blew cold as the wind.

Salter ignored the music, eating his stew noisily and chattering all the while about the herring boats he'd seen at Belinsgate and the orange-capped herringmen, and the tremendous catch they'd brought in.

'It was a fine old sight, Leatherboots. I wish you'd seen them boats comin into the wharf. Handled better than any craft I ever seen. I'd give me eye teeth *and* me toenails to sail a day with them Hollanders!'

While Salter talked, Moss peeped from behind her stew bowl at the bustle that filled The Crow and Stump. It was a very different crowd to the one she'd grown used to at home. Back in the village, The Nut Tree was smoky and busy, but the babble always hummed gently. If the door opened, everyone looked, then got back to their conversations. And Moss had grown to love their talk of harvests and the price of pigs, finding it as comforting as warm milk. Here in The Crow the atmosphere felt charged, like a Tower cannon ready for firing. Conversations moved quickly, eyes were everywhere, and though no one gave a second glance when the door opened, Moss sensed that nobody entered The Crow unnoticed. The people here were not wealthy, she could tell. Their faces were scarred, sinewed and tanned by the sun. And among the browns and greys of their garments were bright sashes, embroidered shawls, feathered hats and beards flashing red ribbons.

'Who *are* all these people?' she murmered.

'Thieves. Pirates. Cutpurses. Cutthroats.' Salter wiped a dribble of stew from his chin. 'Ain't an honest person in here, if that's what yer askin.'

'How do you know that?'

Salter sighed. 'I've been here plenty. When I had business to do, when I wanted somethin that weren't easy to get. And it ain't me favourite place in the world. You'd best keep yer head well down.'

'So you keep telling me.'

But from his corner of the tavern, Eel-Eye Jack's fiddle was singing its sorrowful song. Despite Salter's words of warning, Moss found herself on her feet.

'Leatherboots –'

But Moss was already crossing the tavern to where Eel-Eye Jack stood with one foot raised on a stool, drawing his bow across the walnut fiddle. He was watching her. As she approached he smiled and nodded to the empty chair across the table. She sat and listened while he played the sweet sad end to his tune. Then he lowered his fiddle and sat on his stool, facing her.

'You like this music?'

'Very much. It makes me think of mountains and ice lakes and places I've never seen.'

'You have never been to the cold countries then?' said Eel-Eye Jack.

Moss shook her head.

'Lands of frost and ice, where the mountains are a fine sight, but treacherous too. The falling snow from a mountain can bury a village.'

'Did you live there?' asked Moss.

'Yes. When I was very young.' Eel-Eye Jack rubbed his fingers along the line of his jaw. 'My memories of my country are few but clear. Frozen lakes, boulders of ice. Wolves and white bears.'

'*White bears*? I saw a white bear on the river today. Tethered on a boat. I've never seen such a creature! It was as big as two horses.'

'The great white bear is king among all the animals of my homeland. It can take off a man's head with one bite.'

'Did you ever see one?'

Eel-Eye Jack shook his head. 'I left my country when I was a boy of five. Sailed to England with my mother on a trader's ship. In London we landed and in London we stayed.'

'Oh.' Moss was curious. 'Where is your mother? Is she in London still?'

'My mother is dead. All I have is the memory of her voice calling to me. *Jackin . . .*'

'Jackin? That's your name?'

'*Was* my name. No one calls me that now.'

He stopped. Moss sensed that he had revealed as much about himself as he was prepared to tell.

'So what about you, Moss from-the-village? Moss is a strange name too, perhaps? A name with secrets.'

Moss felt suddenly shy. 'I don't know –'

'Let me try. Tell me if I am right.'

The sweet rhythm of his talk drew her in, soothed her.

'You tell me you are a girl from a village who's never seen a mountain. But you are a girl who knows ice and snow and the bite of a wind that feels as though it will cut you in half. Who knows how to ride underneath a sleigh on a frozen river. Who has seen the inside of a palace –'

Moss's eyes were wide in wonder. 'But how do you know all this about me?' And then she remembered. A year and a half ago. The day the Riverwitch had come. The day Salter had found her in the snow by the side of the river. Eel-Eye Jack's scouts had tracked her.

Eel-Eye smiled. 'There is much to be gained from knowing the movements of others. It pays to have ears and eyes in this city. They watch for me. And yet they can't know a person's thoughts.' He leaned forward. 'I do not know, for example, what you are doing here.'

Moss found herself leaning forward too, lost in

the blue-flame eyes of this boy with his lilting voice.

'Many people pass through The Crow,' he went on. 'I know the usual types of this city and places beyond. But you . . . you do not fit. I would be interested to know more about you, Moss-from-the-village.'

'I'll bet you would.'

Moss wheeled round. Salter was standing behind her. She felt a flush of anger at the interruption.

'Salter, can't you just leave me alone for ten minutes?'

'Come on, Leatherboots –'

'You're not my keeper!'

Salter ignored her. 'Leave her alone, Eel-Eye. She ain't doin nothin fer you.'

'Don't worry, we were just talking. Your friend Moss has a love of music and mountains.'

'Whatever yer up to she don't want no part of it.'

'He's not *up* to anything, Salter!' said Moss. She turned to Eel-Eye Jack. 'I enjoyed talking to you, Jackin.'

'*Jackin?*' spluttered Salter.

Moss gave Salter a shove, hustling him back towards the corner where they'd been sitting before. 'Shut up,' she hissed. 'That's his name.'

'That and a few other things I can think of.'

'What is wrong with you? You're acting like an idiot.'

'No,' said Salter. '*You* are the idiot. You ain't listened to a word I've said since we got here.'

'That's because all you say is don't do this, don't go there, don't talk to him. Honestly, Salter, it's like I'm back in the Tower the way it used to be, with Pa breathing down my neck.'

'I only . . . I just –'

'Well, *don't*. I can look after myself.'

'Look, Leatherboots –'

'And stop calling me that. I do have a name.'

Salter looked confused. 'I thought –'

But Moss had already stomped into the corner and was wrapping herself in her blanket. She hadn't meant to be quite so cross with Salter. But he *was* infuriating. He *was* treating her like a child. And now she thought about it, his nicknames were annoying. Names, words – they mattered.

He was wrong about Eel-Eye Jack, he just didn't like to admit it. Suspicious by nature, he always saw the worst in people. Anyway, wasn't Salter forgetting that the very first time he'd met Moss, he himself had stolen her boots? And yet now, here they were. Friends.

There was always some good in a person, thought Moss. You just had to know where to look.

CHAPTER NINE
On the Roof of The Crow

When Moss woke the next morning, she was surprised to find herself still feeling irritated with Salter. She watched him eating his porridge, shovelling it down as though it might disappear off his plate if he didn't finish it fast enough.

'Eat up then,' he said, scraping the last of the porridge from his bowl. 'Never know where the next meal's comin from.' He sat back and Moss winced as he burped, then wiped his chin on his sleeve. She'd never seen Eel-Eye Jack eat porridge, but she'd bet ten groats that he didn't eat it like that.

Salter seemed to have forgotten the night before. So typical, thought Moss. He'd called her an idiot, if she remembered rightly. Had she called him one first? Maybe she had, but he deserved it, the way he'd carried on while she was talking to Eel-Eye Jack.

'So you walkin again today or what?' said Salter cheerfully, rising from the table.

'I haven't quite decided,' replied Moss. 'But whatever I do, I think I want to be by myself for a bit.'

The cheer in his face vanished. 'By yerself?'

'Yes? What's so strange about that?'

'Nothin, nothin, keep yer hair on. It's just, well, the big city ain't the safest place to go wanderin. With that nice green country dress on you stand out a mile, Leatherboots.'

'I do not. And stop calling me that, can't you?'

'Eh?'

'I told you, I don't like it. And I can look after myself.'

'Oh, fer Harry's sake, go on then, suit yerself! I'll see you later.' And with that, he strode out of the tavern.

Moss watched him go, scratching an itch under the sleeve of her dress. *Don't feel guilty*, she told herself. There were bigger things to think about right now.

Moss sat on the riverbank beside Tower Wharf, scouring the grey water for any sign of the Riverwitch. She'd been sitting there for the best part of an hour and was beginning to wonder if she'd imagined the whole thing. It was entirely possible. Salter always said the river played tricks on your eyes. Five days ago she could have sworn she'd had a conversation with the Riverwitch, but maybe she'd conjured the spirit from some dark place in her mind. The memory of her twelfth birthday, of the desperate grasp of the Witch in the depths of the river. Could memories come back to haunt you?

A sudden wave crashed in front of her and Moss sprang up, startled. As the froth raked back over the pebbles, it left a strand of seaweed that stretched all the way to the water's edge. The waves seemed to have stopped and the river had become eerily calm. In front of her the seaweed jerked, as though something was pulling it.

Moss hesitated. Cautiously she picked up the end of the seaweed. She felt it tug gently so she held it lightly, letting it run through her fingers like string. She followed it all the way to the river's edge. As the water lapped her ankles, she felt the weed tug more urgently, so she let it lead her further, until she was thigh-deep in the river, heading back into the cavernous dark of the wharf.

She stopped by one of the wooden pillars.

Are you there?

Above her, the planks of the wharf creaked. The murky water swilled around her legs, a strange whirling current that made her giddy.

In the darkness, a voice hissed, 'I am here.'

The water slowed and Moss watched as two lantern pools of green rose to the surface.

'You have come as I asked, River Daughter.'

The body of the Riverwitch lay in the water, drifting slightly with the sway of the current.

'Will you make the bargain with me? In return for your freedom.'

'You say my freedom, but what is it you want me to do for it?'

The Witch's lantern eyes clouded. She reached up a ghostly hand, thin as gossamer. It was black from the tips of her fingers to her wrist. It seemed to Moss as if it was rotting away.

'Your hand,' said Moss. 'What's happening to you?'

'The river is choking.'

'Choking?'

'Something is stirring,' said the Witch. 'An ancient evil, once buried deep. My hand, my body, what's left of my soul, this river – all will be consumed by the evil woken from long ago. Soon, all will rot and turn to mud.'

Moss stared at the Witch's blackened fingers.

'You are thinking that if I am destroyed, you need fear me no longer?' The Witch's face split into a hideous grin of fallen teeth and bare bone. 'You are wrong. The river is the blood of the land. If the river dies, men die with it.'

'Why should I believe you?'

'Because you have little to gain if I am lying, and much to gain if I speak the truth.'

'But what can *I* do? I'm just a girl. I don't have power over any ancient evil.'

'Find the one who has woken it. The one who feeds it. Stop him.'

'What? Find who? Stop who? Can't *you* stop him?'

'Him I cannot reach.'

'But who is he? Where is he?'

'He dwells within the walls of the Tower. The Beast House. Many times I have lain in wait. At the steps of the Traitor's Gate. Here, beneath the wharf.

But he knows. He is cunning. He does not come near the water. You must find him. Bring him to me and I will release you from your father's promise.'

The Riverwitch began to sink back into the water. 'Wait! What is his name?'

The Witch's voice was fading. 'All in the Beast House fear him. He is the Under-keeper, the Whipmaster . . .'

And then she was gone, leaving just the slop of water echoing in the darkness.

The tide was coming in fast. Moss waded out from under the wharf and shook out her dress on the bank. The thought of going back there. Inside the Tower. The Tower was a place of death. She couldn't bear it. But what choice did she have? Whatever her horror of the Tower and of the hideous memories waiting to crawl back into her dreams, the thought of a life lived in fear of the Witch coming for her was worse still.

Moss made her way quickly back to the alley and when she got there it was not yet dusk. On an upturned barrel outside The Crow sat Eel-Eye Jack. As he caught sight of her he picked up his fiddle and began to play a skipping rhythm that made her steps feel awkward as she walked towards him.

'Good evening, Moss-from-the-village.'

He stopped playing and stood up. 'Won't you sit with me a while? '

Moss hesitated. 'Is Salter back yet?'

Eel-Eye Jack shook his head. 'Not yet.' He gestured to his barrel seat. 'Come. I'll play for you.'

'I–'

'You can wait for your friend here. It's as good a place as any.'

What harm could it do? thought Moss. She settled herself on the upturned barrel and Eel-Eye Jack took a position below, one leg resting on the tavern step, so that he was looking up at her.

'What would you like me to play? Your choice.'

'I . . . don't know.'

'Something to make your heart dance?' He drew his bow nimbly back and forwards across the strings. 'Or perhaps this bright tune does not match your feeling inside?' He slowed his pace and the walnut fiddle rang with the pure, melancholy sound that had so entranced her the first time she had heard it. As he played, Moss felt the music enfold her, stirring her thoughts, soothing her, and yet all the while filling her with a yearning that she could not place.

'I have often wondered,' said Eel-Eye Jack softly, 'whether sad, beautiful music makes our troubles easier or harder to bear?'

Moss had no answer to this. All she knew was that this was the most wonderful melody she had ever heard.

'Do you sing, Moss?'

'Sing? Well . . . not really.'

'Sing with me. I will play.'

Moss shook her head. 'No, my voice, my notes . . . they're no match for yours.'

'Perhaps you are shy? Out here where people

come and go. But I can show you a place that will make you want to lift your voice to the sky.'

Eel-Eye Jack put out his hand.

Moss looked from his hand to his eyes, wide-blue in a face she could not read.

'Come with me. It won't take a moment. I promise you, you shall not be disappointed.' He took both her hands and lifted her off the barrel to the ground. He led her around the side of the tavern. Clinging to the crooked building was a rickety spiral of steps.

'Up there?' said Moss, gazing at the wooden slats that climbed up and up and disappeared somewhere in the roof of The Crow.

'Follow me,' said Eel-Eye Jack, and he took her slowly up the curling steps until her head was dizzy and she was glad of the steady hand that guided her.

When they reached the top, Eel-Eye Jack scrambled up a thick slope of thatch and Moss found herself following eagerly, drawn by the pink-orange glow that peeked over the rooftop above them.

He pulled her the last few feet. 'There!' he said and Moss gaped in wonder at the sight before her. A rising, falling landscape of rooftops. A hidden world of thatch and tiles and chimneys, shimmering in the haze of the setting sun.

'Oh!' she cried. 'We're as high as the clouds!'

'Almost,' smiled Eel-Eye Jack. 'Let's sit, watch the sunset a while.'

She felt herself wobble with the rush of the high building as they perched on the narrow rooftop.

'I come here when I want to think of faraway things,' said Eel-Eye Jack. 'I imagine the clouds are mountains, the rooftops the dark sea stretching from here all the way back to my homeland.'

Moss listened, lulled by the poetry of his words. Salter never spoke like that.

'Do you miss it?' she asked. 'Will you go back?'

Eel-Eye Jack turned to her. 'Maybe one day. Until then, my music takes me there.' He settled the walnut fiddle under his chin. 'So, Moss-from-the village. I played for you. Will you sing for me?'

'I –'

'There is no one to listen, just the setting sun. Think of yourself on the top of a mountain.'

Moss gazed out at the rooftops. 'I do know a song . . .'

And before she could worry too much about her reedy voice or forgetting the words, Moss found herself singing the song that old Nell had taught her during those long evenings in the Tower. A song that felt as though it came from a lifetime ago, from an old lady who came to warm her peeling feet by the fire and tell her stories of a world Moss thought she'd never see.

Silver river stained with souls
Take care of its depths, my child
When frost and ice creep from her shores
She'll drag you down, my child

As Moss's quiet voice echoed across the rooftops,

she heard the slow, mournful notes of the Hardanger fiddle, lifting her uncertain words, carrying them, as gently as a stream would carry a leaf. She closed her eyes and breathed deeply. Words and notes intertwined, floating together across the sky.

> *A miller's daughter once she was*
> *Spurned on her wedding day*
> *She seeks the thing she'll never have*
> *A loving child to hold*
> *She is the waves, the current strong*
> *The weed that snags your feet*
> *And if she finds you, better drown*
> *Than feel her cold embrace*

Eel-Eye Jack drew the last strokes of his bow and the music dissolved into the fading light. Moss opened her eyes. He was looking at her and the intensity of his gaze filled her with a sudden shyness.

'Why did you come here, Moss?'

The question jerked her back. 'I –' Should she

tell him? He seemed to understand her somehow, to sense her feelings, without really knowing anything much about her. 'I . . . I'm looking for someone,' she said.

'Looking for someone?' said Eel-Eye Jack. 'Here in London?'

Moss nodded.

'Do you have a name for this person?'

Moss shook her head. Eel-Eye Jack put down his fiddle and bow.

'No name makes a search hard, I think.'

Moss's breath caught in her throat. She'd said too much.

'Perhaps I can help you?' said Eel-Eye Jack.

Perhaps he could? thought Moss.

'There's somewhere I need to go.'

'Where?'

'The Tower of London. The Beast House.'

Eel-Eye Jack's cheek twitched. 'The Beast House? The someone you seek, you think you will find them there?'

'I don't know. Perhaps. Will you help me?' she said.

She felt Eel-Eye Jack's blue eyes rake her own. 'I can get you into the Beast House.'

Moss waited. She had the feeling that he was about to add something else.

But all he said was, 'Meet me at the corner of Tower Street. Tomorrow morning, after breakfast.'

Darkness was falling as they scrambled back down the spiral steps. Laughter and shouts spilled from the shuttered windows of The Crow. Moss wondered whether Salter had returned yet. She was glad he hadn't seen her climbing down from the roof with Eel-Eye Jack. She wasn't sure why, exactly. After all, she had nothing to hide. It was just that he was, well, unlike any person she'd ever met. His words were like his music. They soothed her. They transported her to places she could barely imagine. They had awakened something inside her. How could Salter possibly understand that?

CHAPTER TEN
Little Elizabeth

Tower Street really wasn't hard to find. Moss had set off after breakfast with Salter at her heels. The landlord had given her directions and now that she was familiar with the back alleys surrounding The Crow, she felt as though she was beginning to know this part of the city a little better. She'd told Salter who she was meeting and where he was taking her. Of course, Salter had wanted to know why and he'd seemed upset that Moss was asking another favour from Eel-Eye Jack. But she made no mention of the Riverwitch, sticking to the promise she'd made to herself not to get Salter involved.

They stepped on to a wide road bumping with carts. Where the road ended, the carts trundled either left up the hill or down to the river. Straight ahead loomed the walls of the Tower.

'Here it is!' she said, feeling a little flush of satisfaction at finding Tower Street without Salter's help.

'And here *he* is,' said Salter, nodding at Eel-Eye Jack approaching them from an alley that joined the street. In Eel-Eye's hand was one end of a short rope. Twisting around his legs on the other end was a dog.

The dog yapped as Moss approached. It was caked in dirt and tangled up in the rope, as though it had never felt a lead around its neck before.

'Good morning,' said Eel-Eye Jack. He handed the lead to Moss.

'What's this?' said Moss.

'One stray dog,' said Eel-Eye Jack. 'Your payment for entry to the Beast House. Just give it to the men at the Lion Tower gate.'

'That's all I have to do? They'll let me in?'

Eel-Eye Jack nodded. 'You'll see.'

'Thank you,' said Moss.

'Thanks fer nothin,' muttered Salter.

'Don't worry,' said Eel-Eye Jack to Moss. 'Salter knows me and I know him and somehow we find a way to see eye to eye.' He tipped his head at them both and walked off down the road. Salter scowled after him.

'Well, are you coming or not?' Moss tugged the dog and set off along the path. It was just a short walk to the Bulwark Gate where she and Salter found themselves among a straggling queue of people. Many of them had an animal in tow. Moss counted four dogs, two cats, a cage of chickens and a baby goat. She and Salter joined the queue, filing slowly through the gate, and the closer they got, the more Moss could feel her heart hammering in her chest. She didn't even know who she was looking for. *The Under-keeper? The Whipmaster?* That's what the Riverwitch had said. How would she know who he was? Like Salter said, she must be mad as a rabbit trying to get back in to the Tower when she'd spent her whole life wishing herself out of the place. The thought of stepping back into her prison filled her with nausea.

'You all right, Leatherboots?' She felt Salter's hand on her shoulder. 'Let me take that mutt.' He took the rope, untwisting it from her arm. At the gate, the guard looked them up and down.

'The Beast House,' said Moss, more confidently than she felt.

'Just follow the line,' said the guard wearily.

They entered through the Lion's Gate and were hustled along the narrow walkway over the moat. She'd passed this way many times, but only on Execution Days. She shivered. Though she'd done her best to forget that time, as Pa had said she must, the memory still lingered. The baying of the crowd on the Hill, Pa's axe, the blood, a head in her basket. But today the route seemed altogether different. Something had changed though. There was a quietness about the Tower that she could not place.

The Beast House was before them now – a high wall and a wooden gate and the low growl of the animals within.

In front of Moss, a little girl holding a cat began to cry. There was a boy with her, maybe ten years old.

'Shut up, Maudy,' he said.

'But Bramble . . .' She hugged the cat in her arms.

'Don't you want to see the white bear?'

'Yes . . .'

'Then stop crying, can't you?'

As each person passed through the gate, two men wearing leather aprons were taking the animals. Moss scrutinised them carefully. Could either of them be the Under-keeper? How could she tell?

The girl in front let out a wail when they took her cat and dropped it into a wooden crate.

There were some visitors who had no animals and Moss saw these people hand money to the aproned men. She'd always thought the Beast House was closed to all but the keepers and the King himself, but now it seemed it was open to anyone who had either the money or an animal to trade. The men took the dog from Salter, still twisting on its rope and put it in a large crate with several others. Moss looked behind to see a scruffy boy hold up two dead rabbits, only to be shooed away by the men.

'Nothin dead. Live ones only.'

They were in. Standing at one end of an open semi-circular yard. The stench of animal and straw was all around them. Set back in the cavernous walls were arched openings sealed with iron bars. Moss could hear snarls and growls coming from the darkness within. And there were glimpses. The creature they called the tiger, pressing its coat of orange and black striped fur against the bars. A flash of teeth from a grey wolf. A long-necked, mad-eyed bird, pecking at a brick wall. Crowding at the bars of each cell were the people who'd paid to see the beasts. Some hung back, others were bold, peering in for a proper look at a strange and fabulous creature.

At the far end of the yard was an arch larger than the others and it was here that the biggest crowd had gathered. Moss crept among them and began wriggling her way to the front. As she did so, a deep-throated roar thundered from the cell, loud enough to shake the very top of the turrets. There were screams from the crowd and many fell over themselves in the rush to get away from the bars. From the back of the cell, an enormous shape stepped into the light. Milk-white fur, thick as snowfall, streaked with dirt where the beast had lain on the ground. The great white bear was both pitiful and terrifying. The solid trunks of its powerful front legs padded slowly, so that with each step, the bear's lumbering body swayed forward. Around Moss, people began to inch closer. Braver now that the bear was quiet, they laughed and shrieked and exclaimed at its size, the whiteness of its fur, the sharpness of its teeth. The bear snorted, head down. Then it raised its head and for a moment Moss looked straight into its eyes. Orbs of deep brown, blinking in the light. In them Moss saw confusion and rage and the helplessness of an animal far away from anything it knew.

She realised Salter was no longer by her side. Where had he got to? She caught sight of him staring at two grey wolves a few cells down from the bear. There were keepers in the yard, some with brooms, one lowering a bucket of water into the wolves' den through a hatch in the barred door. As Moss watched the wolves lap thirstily at the water, she became aware of someone standing next to her. It was a girl. Slight and pale, her hair was a battlefield of orange curls that stuck out crazily from her head. She could not have been more than four or five years old, yet she wasn't gasping and gawping like the people around her. She stood quite still, her dark eyes locked on the white bear. And when the bear growled, she didn't flinch.

Over the heads of the crowd came the voice of a woman.

'Elizabeth! Child! Where are you?'

The girl darted behind a portly lady and when she saw Moss looking at her, she put her finger to her lips.

'Don't tell her I'm here. Please.' Her voice was clear and bright, her words clipped, like those of a child brought up in a well-to-do house. A little odd, thought Moss, as the girl's clothes were quite plain.

A young woman struggled through the crowd, blustering with the effort of pushing a path through the crush of people.

'Shhh!' The girl peeked from her hiding place. 'Don't let Champers find me. I don't want to go back yet.'

Moss smiled. This little girl was just playing. A game of hide-and-seek. The village children did the very same and Moss would often help them, stuffing them into an apple barrel or concealing them in a pile of straw. She sidled up to the stout lady and lifted the back of her voluminous cloak, so gently that the lady did not even turn round. Then she gestured for the girl to go under. The girl crouched, ducking under the curtain of wool, just as Champers squeezed through the crowd.

'Have you seen a little girl? This high. Red-haired.'

Moss shook her head. 'No, sorry.'

The woman looked flustered. 'Bother! She can't have gone far.' She pressed on through the crowd.

Moss lifted the edge of the cloak. 'She's gone. You can come out now.'

The girl crawled out and Moss couldn't help but laugh at the sight of this feisty little person with a head of hair to match. The girl fixed her berry-brown eyes on Moss. 'It was stuffy under there,' she said, 'but it fooled Champers! Which way did she go?'

'Over there, I think,' said Moss.

'Thank you.' The little girl blinked. Her eyes were familiar somehow.

'I like Champers,' said the girl. 'She's kind to me.'

'Is she?' said Moss, not really knowing why they were having this conversation.

'Yes she is. I begged her to let me come and see the bear. And she said yes! Lady Bryan would *never* have let me. Did you come to see the white bear too? It's a *he*. Champers told me so. She says the bear is from Norway.' Her eyes widened, 'That's a *really* long way away.'

What a strange little girl this was, thought Moss. Talking ten-to-the-dozen in a manner that seemed way beyond her years.

'How old are you?' asked Moss.

'Four-and-a-half,' said the girl. 'Did you know, three hundred years ago, there was another white bear in the Tower? Champers told me that too. It was a present from the King of Norway. Did you know that they used to let the bear swim in the river on the end of a long chain?'

Moss shook her head. 'No, I didn't know that.'

'Well they did. It swam in the river and it caught salmon. Champers says white bears are from the cold countries. They like ice and snow and they are very, *very* dangerous. Champers said not to get too close, but I am not afraid.'

Inches from the bars of the bear's cell, Moss could see that she was not. The bear shook his black snout, puffs of mist snorting from his nostrils.

'I will come again and see you.' The little girl was talking to the bear. 'I am not afraid of you.' Moss had the strange feeling that she was not just talking about the bear, but about something else. 'I do not like this place though.' The girl looked up at the high walls of the Beast House. 'Champers says it is a prison. For animals and for people.'

'Is Champers your aunt?'

'No, she's my governess,' said the girl. 'Instead of Lady B. And I'm glad, because now I can have some fun. Lady B was *so* strict and my half-sister Mary is *so* serious. Mary is twenty-one years old, so she's practically an old lady!'

'Oh.'

'She prays a lot,' added the girl. 'She prays for

me. And she prays for my mother's soul, because my mother is actually dead.' The little girl said this in a matter-of-fact sort-of way, as though she was telling Moss that she liked plums or that her favourite colour was blue.

'Was she ill?' asked Moss.

'I don't know if she was ill.' The girl looked around, as if to check no one was listening. 'Lady B said not to talk about her. She said I should forget her.' The girl looked suddenly crestfallen. 'I don't really remember her. I wish I did.'

It didn't seem quite right to put her arm around a girl she'd only just met, but Moss suddenly felt the urge to do so.

Instead she said, 'What about your father?'

The girl folded her arms and said crossly, 'My father is too busy to see me. But Champers says maybe, some day . . .' Her dark eyes lit up a little. 'Now the baby is born.'

'There you are!' A firm arm gathered up the little red-haired girl and gave her a fierce hug followed

131

by an even fiercer telling-off. 'Oh, my goodness me! Child, you mustn't run off like that. How am I to look after you if you scamper off like a rabbit?'

'Sorry, Champers.' The girl shot a furtive smile at Moss.

'And put your cape on for heaven's sake. It may not be the finest wool but at least it'll keep out this miserable damp.'

Champers did not stay cross for long. She had a kind face, Moss thought, and this little girl with no mother and a father too busy to see her could do a lot worse than to be looked after by a lady with a fierce hug who dressed her warmly and told her about bears.

The governess gathered her skirts and, as if remembering some distant formality said, 'Come now, my Lady Elizabeth, it is time to go.'

The mischief vanished from the girl's face. 'Why won't you call me my Lady Princess?'

The governess crouched down so she could look the girl in the eyes. 'It is hard for you to understand, but no more *Princess*, my little one. You are just my Lady now. The same as your sister.' She sighed and stood up. Then she took the little hand in hers and for a moment the girl looked like any other four-year old. Small and lost.

Moss watched them walk into the crowd.

Princess . . . she thought. *Princess?* Why would she ask to be called that? Only a daughter of a king would be called Princess.

Moss's jaw dropped. A King's daughter?

She stared as the battlefield curls disappeared through the arch of the courtyard. *I gave him a daughter. My little Elizabeth. My little princess redhead . . .* Words spoken long ago in a snow-covered garden. Words spoken by the child's mother. The dead queen. Anne Boleyn.

CHAPTER ELEVEN
Whipmaster

After the Beast House, Salter had asked if Moss wanted to go with him to Belinsgate, but she'd said no. She wanted a little time to take in all that had happened that morning. Now she was back at The Crow, tucked in the corner by the fire, wishing for the quiet of the forge. The thought of it pricked her conscience. Would Pa be worried? It was several days since she'd left the village.

The silver bird lay cupped in Moss's hands. She turned it slowly, stroking the tight wings welded to its body. It had been given to her by Anne Boleyn that day in the snow-covered garden, Moss shivering in a cloak of swan feathers. She recalled the Queen's spirited words. *I say what I think and I make people laugh with my wit.* How un-queenlike she'd seemed. She'd told Moss about her daughter. *My beautiful Elizabeth. My little princess redhead, whom I love more than my own life.*

Moss thought about the girl's brown-berry eyes. Just the same as her mother's. This girl was full of spark and she was tough. She would have been little more than two years old when the Queen was executed. And from the sound of it, she had no idea what had happened to her mother. No one had told her. Perhaps they thought she was too young to understand? Yet the little girl seemed to have a wisdom way beyond her years. Moss knew all too well that painful feeling of *wanting to know*. Of wanting someone so badly, even though they were beyond reach. Did Elizabeth know *anything* about her mother? If she did, chances were that none of it would be good. People said only cruel things about Anne Boleyn.

Moss touched the dagger-sharp beak of the bird. It had saved her life once, and she would always remember the lady who had given it to her. Maybe Elizabeth did not miss her mother now, thought Moss, but one day she would. She slipped the silver bird back into her pocket.

Salter was sitting at a table, devouring a plate of bread and something that vaguely resembled meat. On the other side of the room, Eel-Eye Jack was hunched over a table, talking with a man whom Moss recognised as the same blunt-framed figure from a couple of nights back. Although his face was hidden by the shadow of the stairway, his body was turned slightly towards the room. He was not a big man, yet there was something powerful in the way he held himself. He rose slowly, scraping his chair. As he did so, he dropped a mutton bone. On the floor right in front of Eel-Eye Jack. Sly eyes glanced. Moss felt a ripple running through the chatter of the tavern. There was something menacing about the way the man had dropped that bone, the way he'd let it slide from his hand to the floor. He made his way across the room, the packed crowd parting to let him through. It seemed no one wanted to get in his way.

'Come an' eat. You must be starvin.' Salter was standing before her now, holding out a hand to help her up.

Moss shook her head. 'I'm not hungry,' she said.

Salter dropped his hand and sat down on the floor next to her. 'You got to eat, Leatherb-' then he checked himself. 'You got to eat, that's all.'

'Maybe later.'

What now, thought Moss? She'd been to the Beast House, she'd talked to a princess, she'd seen a great white bear, but she hadn't found the person she was looking for. The Under-keeper. The Whipmaster. She would just have to go back.

Moss pushed off her blanket and stood up.

'Hungry now?' said Salter.

'No, there's just something –'

Quick as a lick, Salter was up and by her side.

'Don't,' he said.

'Don't what?'

'Don't get tangled up with Eel-Eye Jack.' He moved in front of her, as if to block her way.

'I'm not getting tangled up with anyone. Let me pass, Salter.'

Salter's face was close to hers. 'Please. Listen to me. You can't trust him.' But Moss wriggled past before he could finish.

She walked over to where Eel-Eye Jack was sitting on his stool, head bent, fingers tightening the strings of his fiddle.

'Jackin, can we talk?'

Eel-Eye Jack looked up. The skin around his eyelids was ringed with shadow.

'Tell me, Moss-from-the-village, did you see what you wanted to see today in the Beast House?'

'Well . . . I don't know.'

'You do not know?'

'It's complicated.'

Eel-Eye Jack ran his fingers down the strings. 'There are many who like to live a simple life. But I think you are not one of them?'

Moss did not reply. It was as though this boy could see into the jumbled mess inside her head.

'You have something to ask me?' he said.

She nodded.

'You want my help again perhaps?'

'I think so.'

'But you are not sure? Perhaps your friend Salter has warned you of me. Perhaps he has told you things about me?'

'No –'

'Nothing?'

'He just said that –' The boy's gaze seemed to draw the words from her mouth. 'He said, that we shouldn't ask a favour from you. That you weren't his friend. He said –' She stopped again, caught by the blue-flame eyes that made her want to speak the things that should stay unspoken. 'He said that you are not to be trusted.'

Her words hung in the space between them.

'And what do *you* think?' said Eel-Eye Jack.

'I think, I don't know. I think that I have no choice.'

'No choice can make a girl bold.'

Eel-Eye Jack picked up his fiddle and tucked it under his chin. 'I knew a bold girl once,' he said. 'A girl I met here in this city. Although she was not from here. She came on a boat, from a land far away.'

'Like you,' said Moss.

'Like me. But not like me. She was wild. She was my friend. But we argued one night and she ran away.'

'What happened to her?'

'She did a reckless thing. And now . . .' Eel-Eye Jack stopped. 'Tell me, Moss, what are you here for?'

That question again.

'I need to go back again,' said Moss, 'To the Beast House.'

'Then you need another dog.'

Moss swallowed. She'd guessed what all the

animals were for. They were food for the beasts.

'Where do you get them from?' she said.

Eel-Eye Jack cocked his head to one side, as though reading her thoughts. 'Strays,' he said. 'Lost ones. Hungry ones with nowhere to go. The Beast House is a quick death for a stray that would starve in a cold winter. And they get a fine meal from me before they go.'

He pulled his bow across the fiddle and a note, clear as a stream, echoed to the rafters, followed by another and another. Eel-Eye Jack looked at Moss while he played, threading his necklace of sorrowful notes, and she felt the music settle inside her, a balm for her troubled thoughts.

The next day, Salter ate a hurried breakfast and made to leave the tavern alone. When Moss asked him where he was going, he replied, 'To see the fishermen,' but would say no more than that. The crinkle was gone from his eyes. Moss could see something was troubling him and she guessed he was cross that she'd talked with Eel-Eye Jack again. It could not be helped though, and she watched him go, resolved to think no more about it.

Later, Eel-Eye Jack had returned to the tavern with another stray. A limping mutt on the end of a short piece of rope. The dog had no bark and didn't look well enough to last a mild autumn, never mind a cold winter. Perhaps he was right. A quick death was better than a lingering one.

'Thank you,' she'd said, and Eel-Eye Jack had replied by pressing a small cloth bundle into her hand. She'd unwrapped it as she'd left the tavern. It was a leg of chicken, freshly cooked, but she had no appetite so she wrapped it up again and put it in her pocket.

It was well into the afternoon by the time Moss reached the Tower. The yard was a crush of people. Laughing and excited and all shoving in the direction of the large arch on the far side. Word must have spread about the great white bear. Moss craned her neck to see if she could see any keepers, but squashed by the crowd, it was all she could do to stay on her feet. Thick cloaks, padded doublets, burly shoulders pressed her from all sides. Everyone was pushing to get a glimpse. She ducked her head to protect herself and burrowed through the forest of legs.

'This is ridiculous!' Moss could hear the keepers yelling. 'Tell the gate guards not to let any more through!'

As the pushing got rougher and the shrieking louder, the animals began to stir and soon the yard was drowning in a wave of howling wolves and growling lions. Then, louder than all the rest, battering the high walls of the Beast House, came a strangled roar. For a moment it silenced the yard and then –

CRASH!

Gasps from the crowd. Another crash. Of metal on stone. Then the screaming started. All around Moss, people began to panic. Bodies twisted in all directions, scrambling for the gate.

'The bear! The bear! It's breaking out!'

The crush of the crowd tumbled Moss to her knees. Instinctively, she curled herself into a ball, shielding her face with her arms and tucking her legs in as tight as she could, while her back was trodden and kicked by stampeding feet. She couldn't stay here. She'd be trampled to death.

She crawled, inching towards a wall where at least she could take refuge until some of the crowd had gone. Many times she cried out at the kick and stamp of boots on her back. She reached the wall and struggled to her feet. But to her horror, she felt the crush of the crowd against her whole body, flattening her against solid stone, squeezing the air from her chest. Her head reeling, she clawed her way along until she felt the bars of one of the animal arches. The den was dark and the floor littered with straw, but it appeared to be empty. On one side of the barred door was a small hatch. It was a feeding hatch, the same as the one she seen the keepers use the day before. Dizzy and breathless, Moss tugged at it. To her surprise it opened. It was a crazy thought, but maybe, if she could get through the hatch, she could just hide there until the panicking crowd cleared.

Headfirst, she squeezed her body through the small square gap, wrenching her shoulders this way and that, wrestling herself through. The rest of her body followed, dropping like a newborn calf on to the floor of the den.

Inside was a musky animal smell, but no sight or sound of any beast. The cell was long and dark with a barrel-shaped roof. Moss crawled to the back and tucked herself into a corner. Her head was pounding. Outside, people were still screaming. Through the din, Moss heard the shouts of the keepers.

'Bring the irons! The irons! Now!'

From her hiding place she could see through the barred arch at the front of the den. The crowd was thinning and she could just make out the white bear's cell across the yard. The bear was throwing himself against the bars. No wonder people were running. The door shook, the chains that held it creaked and stretched, and Moss could see that there was no way that door could withstand a battering from the strength of such a creature.

CRASH!

The chains snapped and the iron-barred door fell to the ground. There was an almighty roar and the bear lumbered out.

The keepers rushed forward with red-hot iron rods.

'Back! Back!' they cried, thrusting the rods towards the bear.

This only seemed to make the bear more wild. With a giant paw he swiped at the rods, sending one of them flying from the hands of a keeper, knocking the man to the ground. The bear roared and lifted the weight of his body up on to two feet, towering above the crowd. The keepers cried out in terror and staggered backwards. For a moment the bear stayed there, swaying on two legs, claws arcing from the pads of giant forepaws, lips stretched taut across dagger-sharp teeth.

'Stay where you are.' A voice cut through the cries.

Striding across the yard was a man, laced and strapped into a beaten coat of tough leather. In one hand he held a whip. In the other was a flaming torch, which he brandished like a sword, swiping this way and that in front of the bear. The creature roared, shaking his muzzle. His cry was more terror than anger, thought Moss, as though he feared the bite of the flames. The leather man unfurled his whip and it crick-cracked through the air like lightning, striking the bear on his snout.

The animal howled in pain and crashed to all fours.

'White beast, get back!' snarled the man. His voice held a crude power that made Moss curl tighter in her corner. Making sure his gaze never left the animal, he yelled to the keepers, 'Open the old bear den!' He thrust the burning torch forward and the bear recoiled. 'Do it. Now!'

The keepers rushed across the yard to the very cell where Moss was crouching and tore the barred door open, holding it wide. Moss shrank back into the darkness and watched, helpless, while more keepers herded the bear towards her. She knew that she should shout, let them know she was in there. She opened her mouth to cry out, but her voice stuck in her throat. The giant bear lumbered through the open door, black mouth scraped back to a snarl. Moss could not move.

The man with the whip goaded the bear forward. The keepers were at his flanks, poking with the red-hot iron rods. Once more the whip cracked through the air, slicing into the bear's ear. The bear yelped.

'You shall know who your master is.'

Though the bear could not possibly understand the man's words, Moss sensed that he grasped their brutal meaning well enough. The great head dropped from his shoulders and he shuffled forward until he was inside the den. At the back, in the dark, tight as a ball of twine, Moss did not move. The keepers slammed the door shut and dragged chains from one side to the other.

In front of her, the great white bear slumped to the floor with a noise that seemed to come from deep within. Moss pressed herself as far back in her corner as she could. The enormous bear rolled over and lay motionless on his side, eyes half-closed. His ear was bleeding, soaking pink-red into his fur. The animal looked utterly defeated.

Out in the yard, the man coiled his whip and fixed it to a wide belt around his tunic. *The Whipmaster*, whispered Moss to herself, no doubt in her mind.

She saw him stride out and noticed the keepers keeping their distance, as though they feared this man almost as much as the raging bear.

The yard was empty now, save for the keepers gathering up fallen hats and shoes. Over the high walls of the Beast House, dusk was settling. She heard the gate clang. All was quiet.

Still the white bear did not move. He was breathing deeply, one forepaw flopped over the other, his back rising and falling with each breath. His head was smooth, as though it had been brushed with a fine comb. Occasionally his nose twitched, but his half-closed eyes were still as stone and Moss could not tell whether the animal was awake or asleep. His body filled the entire width of the cell between Moss and the hatch in the door. She stared at his feet and counted five crescent-shaped claws, blade-sharp, long enough to slice her flesh to the bone. This creature could kill her as easily as look at her. Yet there was something vulnerable too. Locked away in the damp and dark of the Tower. Moss had seen how the Tower could crush a man's spirit. This bear had only been a prisoner for two days and already it was as though he was breaking.

What now? Sooner or later the bear would sense her. He would wake up and most likely attack her.

The only way out was the way she'd come in – through the feeding hatch. Trouble was, there was an enormous bear now lying in the way. To reach the hatch, she would have to climb over him.

Moss began to creep forward, trying to make as little noise as possible as her hands and knees scuffed the stone floor. She could see the bear's hind paws stretched out behind his body. She was close now. Close enough to see the hairs above the bear's lips twitch.

Close enough to see the bear's eye slowly open.

Instantly Moss froze. The eye swivelled in its socket and trained itself on Moss. She was just a few feet away, rooted to her hands and knees.

The bear raised his head. Alert, ears forward, nostrils flared. He rolled off his side on to his stomach and placed his weight on two hefty forepaws. Both eyes were now wide open. Blinking at Moss. Watching her every move.

From nowhere came the memory of Old Samser's dog Poppy, and the way she crouched low and bent her head when the big dogs from the farm came prowling into The Nut Tree with Farmer Bailey. So Moss bowed her head like Poppy and scrunched herself low to the ground, hoping to goodness the bear would think her harmless and not attack. For a few moments she dared not look. All she could hear was the bear's rough breath. But the creature did not move. She raised her eyes slightly. He was looking straight at her, sizing her up.

Then she remembered Eel-Eye Jack's chicken leg. Slowly, so as not to startle the bear, she slid her hand into her pocket where she'd stuffed it and pulled off its cloth wrapping. She slid it across the floor towards the bear.

The bear's huge brown eyes swivelled down to the chicken leg. Do bears eat chicken, wondered Moss? Do *white* bears eat chicken?

The bear sniffed the leg. With one swift movement, he closed his jaw around the chicken.

Crunch. It was gone in a gulp.

The bear licked his lips and looked at her, and it occurred to Moss that she had possibly done a really stupid thing. Now the bear was thinking about food. And the only food left in the den was Moss herself.

She decided to try something bold. Gently, Moss held out the back of her hand for the bear to sniff, just the way she did with Poppy. The bear looked at her hand. How delicate his lashes were, she thought, spidery wisps quivering against white fur.

Her hand was inches from the bear's mouth now. She almost daren't breathe. She could see the wide nostrils pulsing, taking in her scent. She hoped her smell was different to the keepers, that he would not think she was one of them. What did she smell of? Smoke perhaps? Riverwater?

Slowly, the bear pushed his nose against Moss's hand. Her fingers buckled, but she stayed as still as she could while the bear nuzzled her. Then Moss felt a rough wetness on her skin. The bear's tongue scraping up down. The creature was licking her. He licked her hand, then the smooth wool of her sleeve, then her shoulder and now she felt the fuzzy roughness on her cheek. Was he *tasting* her? She closed her eyes, praying that this was not what a bear did to its main meal before crunching it to pieces.

The bear stopped licking. Moss opened her eyes. He lay in front of her now, rolling his head and groaning softly. The gashed ear was still bleeding.

Moss had seen Poppy lick her own wounds and she guessed this was what the bear would have done, only he could not reach. He dropped his head to one side, resting on his forepaws.

'Your ear hurts?' said Moss softly. The bear would not understand her, but much as the creature had responded to the brutal Whipmaster, perhaps he would sense that Moss meant no harm.

The bear didn't move.

Moss held out her hand again for the bear to sniff, then slowly moved it across his snout, down his muzzle. Still the bear did not move, just lay with his head on his paws, huge brown eyes blinking at Moss.

'It's all right,' she said. 'I won't hurt you.' She stroked the fur on his neck, taking care to show the bear that her hands were empty. 'I suppose you are a long way from home. The cold countries.' She kept her voice low. 'Mountains and ice . . .'

It felt slightly crazy to be talking to a bear, but the creature moved his head slightly, as if curious to see the place these soothing noises were coming from.

'I've never seen a mountain, but I've walked on ice. It was an ice river. A wide, deep river that flows to the sea.'

The bear grunted.

Moss moved her hand upwards to the tufted fur at top of his head. The bear's bleeding ear twitched. She scrunched the chicken cloth into a ball and pressed it gently against the bleeding ear. The bear whined quietly, but lay quite still while Moss held the cloth to the wound, stemming the oozing blood. She could feel the warmth of the bear's body, rising and falling with deep, tired sighs. Up and down. And gradually she leant her own body against the thick fur. The bear did not seem to mind. His eyes closed and soon enough, lulled by his slow breathing, Moss felt her hand drop and her own eyes closing as sleep carried her far away.

CHAPTER TWELVE
Hiding

She didn't know how long she'd been sleeping, but Moss woke with a start to the clang of the gate. She froze, finding herself surrounded by the creamy white fur of a huge beast. Then she remembered. Gingerly she leant forward to look at the bear. He was still asleep. Out in the yard she could hear the crunch of cartwheels on the cobbles and low voices in the night.

Taking care not to wake the sleeping bear,

Moss clambered to her feet and peeked over the hump of his back.

A covered cart stood in the moonlit yard. Next to it, Moss counted four men and another four by the wolf den. In the midst of them all was the Whipmaster, growling orders.

'Open the cage, Finch.'

'But they don't look asleep, Mr Severs . . .'

'Well they damn well should be! Sully, what did you give them?'

'No food, so they should be hungry. And no water. Just beer. Gallons of the stuff.'

'Beer you say? Idiot! I told you wine!'

'But Mr Severs, sir, the beer is cheaper.'

'And *weaker* you fool! The wolves won't be asleep. Finch! Give Sully the ropes.'

Moss watched the man called Finch hand several lengths of stout rope to Sully.

'Well, Sully, since you've only got half a brain, you won't miss the other half if a wolf bites it out of your head! Now get in that cage and tie them up.'

'But Mr Severs . . .'

'Do as I say, you mangy bag of ratbones!' He patted the whip by his side. 'Or maybe you'd rather feel the bite of leather across your back?'

'No, Mr Severs.'

Sully took the rope and crept into the cage. Moss heard snarling and the snap of teeth from inside the cage.

'Arrgghh!'

Moss watched the Whipmaster snatch a club from the hands of one of the men and stride into the wolf den. She heard a startled whine followed by two swift thuds.

The wolves fell silent.

'Now tie them up and get them loaded on to the cart. We don't have all night.'

The men did as they were told. Two wolves, their feet bound with rope, were dragged out, and with great effort, heaved onto the cart. A large oilcloth was thrown over them. The men set about locking up the den.

Where were they taking the wolves? Wherever it was, Moss had seen her chance. If she could hide in that cart, she could get out.

Moss pulled off her boots and climbed over the sleeping bear as lightly as she could. Pressing herself flat to the stone floor, she crawled to the hatch. The Whipmaster and several of his men were already walking towards the gate. Four others were taking up the shaft of the cart and preparing to heave it over the cobbles.

Quickly, Moss lifted the hatch and squeezed herself out, dropping silently into the yard. The back of the cart was just a few feet from the bear den. Boots in one hand, she flitted across the cobbles in bare feet and crouched behind the wheels. The men yanked the cart from standstill and as it began to move off, Moss lifted the oilcloth and darted on board, hoping the juddering would mask her scuffles.

Now she found herself in total darkness, the reek of wolf and beer all around her. She wedged herself against one side, feeling the furry weight of a wolf lolling beside her. She guessed the Whipmaster had knocked them out cold. But why?

The cart trundled on and stopped at what Moss guessed was the main gate. She heard voices and the chink of coins, then they were off again. She could feel herself tipping forward. They must be going downhill. After a few minutes the cart left the dirt road and she heard the clatter of the wheels on wood. Then it stopped once more and Moss was just about to peek out to see whether she might make her escape, when she felt the cart jerk again.

'Steady!'

'She's on!'

They'd stopped . . . and they hadn't. They were still moving, but side to side, a gentle rocking. Lifting the oilcloth just a chink, Moss peered out. Above her was inky sky and all around the cart, the low sides of a boat. Beyond that, the gentle swell of water, twinkling in the moonlight.

They were on the river!

She guessed they must be on some kind of barge, big and steady enough to take the cart. She could see the men puffing and straining, two to an oar.

'Come on, Sully,' said the man Finch who was sitting next to him. 'Get them weedy little arms of yers workin.'

'Ha ha,' jeered one of the others. 'Sully ain't never been to the Pit before, has he?'

'No, he ain't,' said Finch. 'Hope you didn't have a big supper, Sully. First time in the Pit, it'll likely end up on yer boots.'

'I ain't no gipper,' said Sully. 'How far is this Pit anyway?'

'Three miles to The Dogs, and Severs don't like it if we keep him waitin.'

'Why ain't he comin by boat?'

Finch lowered his voice. 'He don't like the water.'

'Why not?'

'Afraid of it, ain't he.'

'But why? It's just the river.'

'Not to him. They say he's *seen* things.' Finch's eyes darted left and right.

'What things?'

'The Riverwitch. He's seen her eyes. Green lanterns in the murk. Watchin him. An' her hands in the weeds, ready to grab him –'

'Ohhh!' cried Sully, kicking out.

'Stop it, you daft coloppe, that's just a bit of old rope.'

'Ha ha!' laughed one of the others, 'A groat says Sully gips before the night's out.'

Sully went quiet. The others rowed on. Moss lowered the oilcloth and began to wonder whether she shouldn't have just taken her chances back in the bear den. Stayed there and sneaked out in the morning. How would she ever get back from wherever it was they were going? The *Pit* they'd called it. She thought back to the Witch's words under Tower Wharf. *Something is stirring. An ancient evil, once buried deep. Find the one who has woken it . . .*

In her head had been a half-baked plan to make

a dash for it the first chance she got. But now she'd found the Whipmaster. She must stay on the cart. Stay hidden. Find out what the Whipmaster was doing with a cartload of wolves in the middle of the night. Find a way to bring him to the Riverwitch.

It was some time before she felt the lurch of the boat hitting dry land.

She peeped from under the cloth. They were beached on a flat muddy shore. In front of her, as far as the eye could see was mud and marsh. To her left was a high walkway – a rickety bridge hewn from rough planks that ended in a broad platform, supported by great pillars of wood driven deep into the marsh. Across the bridge strode Severs. He stopped on the platform, surveying the marsh, gesturing to some men who scuttled down a ramp from a lower level underneath the bridge. Moss saw them throw planks of wood down on to the mud and felt the cart move forward and up. She could hear gasps from the men as they shoved from behind.

Dropping back down under the cloth, Moss felt the cart trundle along the lower level of the bridge. There was a muffled growl next to her and she felt the wolf move. She pressed herself tightly against the side of the cart, hoping they'd get to wherever they were going quickly. Above the crack of cartwheels, she could hear another noise. Distant but growing, like a wave. The clamour of a crowd. Louder now. She felt the cart speed up as though rolling down a slope. Then they stopped.

'OPEN THE GATE!'

They had arrived. And now Moss knew she had to get off this cart quick before the men began to unload their cargo. One last peek over the side and she could see that the men were right there, standing, waiting. She wriggled round and lifted the cloth where her feet had been. At the back of the cart there was no one. This was her chance. Slipping silently down, she landed on the slatted bridge and crept behind a pillar. Though the moon was out, it was dark enough to hide away in the shadows.

She was pretty sure no one had seen her.

In front of her was a gate set into a high sloping wall that looked like it was made of earth or mud. From behind the wall came the noise of many people.

At that moment the gate opened to let the cart through and Moss caught a glimpse of a fiery light within. She watched Severs stride in, followed by the men pulling the cart. The gate closed and she was alone.

Sliding down the pillar into the mud, she walked backwards to get a better look. The wall was as tall as a forest oak and sloped inwards. Whatever this structure was, it seemed to be circular. It looked like a giant upturned bowl with an open top. She began to walk around it, keeping her distance, sticking to the shadows. The mud was sticky beneath her feet and, as she struggled through, she caught the rising stench of rot and decay. She crept a little closer to touch the wall. The earth was densely packed and shored up with crude timbers. As she stared up at it, a thought occurred to Moss.

This was a wall she could climb.

Digging her boots into the earth, Moss began to scramble up. It wasn't easy to get a foothold, but the wooden struts helped and she splayed herself flat like a spider, spreading her weight against the slope. The higher she climbed, the louder grew the noise within. Several times her feet slipped and she found herself sliding, fingers clawing, cheek skimming the mud. By the time she was halfway up, Moss was caked in the stuff, head to toe. Perhaps it was no bad thing, she thought. This way she was less likely to be spotted.

The noise was deafening now. The cries of many people shouting as one. Almost there. Just a few more feet. Her hands patted a flat lip of earth.

Slowly, Moss pulled her head up and looked over the top of the wall.

CHAPTER THIRTEEN
The Pit

Below her, lit by a hundred flaming torches, was a blazing, shrieking Hell.

An enormous pit. Row upon row of circular terraces, hollowed out from the thick mud wall and shored up with wooden planks. On these terraces stood hundreds of people – shouting, spitting and drinking. They barely seemed human, their features contorted, flushed with a frenzied look that was not anger or fear. It was a look Moss had seen before. On the faces of those who'd come for the executions on

Tower Hill. Bloodlust. A cry for suffering and death.

Every eye was trained on the arena below. On one side were two hefty wooden gates, closed to the world outside. On the other, a smaller wicker gate with an open passage behind it. In the arena itself men were dragging what looked like dead dogs across the earth floor, stuffing them into sacks and hauling them out through the wicker gate. A cry went up, a chant. Low at first, gathering strength until it exploded, a savage chorus pounding the night sky.

'Beasts! Beasts! BEASTS!'

Then she spotted him. The Whipmaster. Astride what looked like a throne of packed mud strewn with animal skins. She ducked as his eyes raked the Pit, his body motionless on the terrace where he sat. It was as though he was made of iron. His face crackled in the torchlight. Hard as armour, with a pitiless gaze that could run a man through.

She turned her attention back to the arena. The pair of grey wolves were being dragged in through the wicker gate. Their feet were still bound and the men waited for a signal from the Whipmaster before cutting the ropes. The crowd jeered and booed until more men hurried in, carrying buckets of water, which they threw over the wolves. Startled by the cold water, the wolves staggered to their feet. They shook their shaggy coats and snarled at the men, who backed away quickly, shutting the gate behind them.

Now the crowd began a new chant.

'Wolf Fight! Wolf Fight!'

Another signal from Severs and, from the corner of her eye, Moss saw a flash of red. A small figure sprang from the high terrace into the arena. Skinny-limbed and barefoot, the figure darted towards the wolves. It was a boy, dressed in dirt-brown breeches and a short tunic of rust-red leather. His head was bound with a piece of cloth, knotted at the back like a scarf. Across his eyes he wore a leather mask.

One of the grey wolves lunged and the boy leapt high, twisting his body to avoid its snapping jaws. But as he turned, Moss saw that he wore his hair braided in two long plaits. She screwed up her eyes, craning to see in the darkness. The boy jumped up, back on to the first tier of the high terrace and for a few moments his masked face was lit by the glow of the flickering torches.

That was no boy, it was a girl! She couldn't have been much older than Moss herself, small in stature with a slender face and a mouth set in eager determination. She had no weapons, or none that Moss could see. And her tunic gave her little protection. What was she going to do? Fight the wolves with her bare hands?

The wolves stood on one side, growling. They didn't look particularly ready for a fight. Moss swung her gaze back to the girl. As light-footed as a deer, the girl ran around the lip of the high terrace, down the sloping mud wall and with a single bound she sprang from behind the wolves, landing on the ground right in front of them. The shock of her sudden arrival startled the beasts and they flew at her, tearing at the air. But she was quick. Darting this way and that, she changed direction so swiftly that the wolves missed her, snapping at her bare heels as she leapt out of their way. She scrambled back up the mud wall to the terrace.

Now the animal snarls were drowned by the roar of the crowd, urging the girl back into the fight. With a graceful jump, she turned a complete somersault high in the air and landed square in the centre of the arena. The wolves, wiser this time, prowled around her, one on each side. They padded slowly, teeth bared, black mouths dripping, their circle getting tighter. And Moss held her breath, for she could see the girl had no way past them and she was nowhere near a wall. The wolves had her trapped.

With a full-throated roar, the wolves threw themselves at the girl. As the gaping jaws of one closed around her leg, at the last moment she whipped it free, bounding on to the wolf's snout and running the length of its back before launching herself into the air. Time seemed to slow. The girl spread her arms, her body stretched, soaring through the air like a bird, in a graceful arc.

The crowd gasped. Moss stared, her mouth dropped in wonder. For a moment she thought the girl was flying.

Soft as a cat, the girl landed on the ground behind the wolves, and ran up the wall to the terrace.

The crowd cheered and began to chant.

'JEN-NY WREN! JEN-NY WREN! JEN-NY WREN!'

Jenny Wren . . . A girl with wings, thought Moss. She wondered how such a girl had ended up in a place like this.

The wolves had shaken off their torpor and were now fully alert. Enraged by the girl who seemed just a snap away, they ripped at her, always missing by a hair's breadth. But Moss could see the girl was growing tired. Her leaps were shorter, her twists and turns slower. Now she was scrambling up the wall, right beneath the mud throne where Severs sat. She crouched there, panting. Moss saw her look up at the Whipmaster, as though pleading to stop. He stood and a hush fell upon the crowd of the Pit. A smile split the Whipmaster's face. With a flick of his boot, he tipped the girl from the wall.

Moss gasped as the girl slid into the arena. The wolves tore towards her. The Pit roared. This is what they had come for. Their chants grew savage. Quick as a rabbit, the girl rolled to the side and sprang to her feet. She dashed madly for the nearest piece of wall and hauled herself up, the wolves raging at her heels.

Across the arena, the lightning crack of a whip silenced the crowd once more. It was a signal. Jenny Wren's performance was over. The girl bowed and made her way along the terrace and dropped out of sight behind the wicker gate.

Moss had barely caught her breath when Severs cracked his whip once more.

'BRING OUT THE DOGS!'

The crowd cheered. From somewhere behind the gate came the braying of dogs. Then the gate burst open and into the arena they piled, a howling mass of teeth that set upon the wolves, leaping for their necks. The terrified wolves fought back, trying to shake the dogs from their fur where they hung, jaws clamped tight as steel traps.

The Whipmaster rose again from his throne and cracked his whip. A dozen men strode into the arena, brandishing clubs and torches to beat the dogs back through the gate.

One wolf lay on the floor, unmoving. The other was slumped beside it, licking its wounds.

Surely that must be the end, thought Moss. These wolves could fight no more.

But the Pit was working up yet another chant. The inner gate opened once more. Through it was pushed a man. In one hand he held a club. In the other, a knife. He staggered forward. A whip crick-cracked through the air. All the men with torches rushed the wolves, goading one to its feet before backing from the arena. The wolf and the man faced each other from opposite sides of the ring.

'FIGHT! FIGHT!' screamed the crowd.

Moss could watch no more. Swallowing a cry, she

scrambled away from the lip of the Pit. Back down the wall she slid, hitting the ground and feeling her legs buckle. She had to get away. The terrible sights she'd seen on Tower Hill were nothing compared to this. Death was a sport to these people. She could barely believe they *were* people. A ravening pit of devils who shrieked for blood.

She staggered back across the deserted bridge. The empty barge rocked in the water. She crept down the planks to the shore and on to the boat, where she threw herself among a pile of sacks at the far end. She guessed that if the wolves survived they'd be taken back on the boat to the Tower. Once the boat was moored at the wharf, she could make her escape.

She was shaking, seized by the shock of all she'd seen. Things she wished she could un-see. The frightened, frenzied animals. The pleading face of the girl. The man made to fight. And the one who controlled the whole appalling spectacle. The vicious, brutal Whipmaster.

CHAPTER FOURTEEN
Catching Salmon

The candles were out at The Crow. The alley was so dark that Moss had to practically feel her way down it. She didn't care. There could be a thousand demons lurking in that alley, but none would haunt her as much as the things she'd just seen in the Pit.

She almost tripped over the body huddled on the doorstep of the inn.

'Pope's Knuckles! Where you been all this time, Leatherboots? I been lookin everywhere!'

'Oh, Salter!'

She collapsed on the step next to him and felt his arm pull her gently towards him. She felt like sobbing, but no tears would come. Instead she just leant her head against his shoulder.

Salter didn't ask any more questions. They stayed on the step for a while, until eventually he touched her cold hand, pulled her to her feet and steered them both inside.

Eel-Eye Jack was in his corner. Moss didn't see it, but she supposed Salter had shot him some kind of glowering look as they entered, because he said nothing, just dipped his head as if to bid them goodnight.

Over the days that followed, Moss kept all she'd seen in the Pit to herself. She half-wished Salter would ask her again where she'd been, but he didn't. Wasn't he interested at all in why she'd been so upset that night? Didn't he care? She found herself wondering whether Eel-Eye Jack might make a better person to confide in, though she realised she'd hardly seen him these past days. The Crow and Stump was empty without his music and, in the silence, Moss found her thoughts turning more and more to Pa. He'd be anxious by now, she was sure of it. The thought of him alone, and sick with not knowing, made her want to get up and leave. But what good would that do, if she spent the rest of her days living in fear of the Riverwitch? She had to stay. At least *try* and finish what she had begun. So she spent her time by the river, close to Tower Wharf, wishing she could think of a way to deliver the Whipmaster to the Riverwitch. She tried to shut out the whispering voice that told her what a hopeless task she faced. Such a cruel and powerful man. It was impossible.

Autumn was now heavy in the air. Smoke and the crackle of leaves and a chill that came one cloudless night and never left. Moss had always savoured the shivery days before the real cold set in. A fire in autumn could warm your bones. But once the frost and fog of winter arrived, you stayed cold until spring.

This autumn though, something was different. After the cheers and bonfires and church bells ringing all over London for the birth of the new Prince Edward, London had gone quiet. Moss heard the whispers and the gossip, from the tavern all the way to the river. Queen Jane was ill. For three days now, she had lain in her bed at Hampton Court with a fever. And a fever after childbirth was a dangerous thing. Moss knew that.

The whispers grew.

'They say she's paler than posset.'

'With a fever hot enough to boil an egg.'

'She lost so much blood – enough to fill a bucket is what I heard.'

'Three days labouring with that child, no wonder!'

'And the boy?'

'Healthy as a country pig. Though the King keeps him swaddled and his rooms swabbed and won't let a cough within a hundred miles of the palace.'

Each day Moss saw less and less of Salter. He would disappear, leaving before breakfast, returning after supper. She supposed he didn't want to take any more favours than he had to from Eel-Eye Jack, but whatever he was getting up to, he kept it to himself. She knew Salter often preferred his own company, but couldn't imagine what he was doing out there from dawn to dusk. She'd tried asking, but he'd just winked and dashed off. It was so typical of him, thought Moss. Hide everything. Reveal nothing. At the back of her mind, a suspicious little seed grew. Was he stealing? Scamming? Was this what he'd missed about his life in London? She tried to shake the bad thoughts from her head. There was no reason to suppose he'd gone back to his old ways. She flushed with guilt for even thinking it.

But the thoughts wouldn't go away, so that morning she woke early, watched Salter shovel down his porridge and as soon as he'd gone through the door, she scrambled from under her blanket and followed him. Darting in and out of doorways, she shadowed him as best she could. He walked fast and the lanes were so busy, she could not let him get more than a few yards ahead or she'd lose him. More than once, his tousled head disappeared and she ran full pelt down an alley to catch up, skidding to a halt when she rounded a corner and saw him striding just a few paces ahead.

When he reached the shore of the river, he crunched on to the shingle and finally stopped. Moss leapt behind an upturned boat and crouched down with her back to the wood. She waited a few seconds before carefully raising her head over the top.

'Oh! For goodness sake!' she cried and stumbled backwards. Salter's face grinned back at her from the other side of the boat.

'Ha ha! You ain't no shadow, Leatherboots,' chuckled Salter. 'Got about as much stealth as a barrel rollin down a hill!'

Moss picked herself up from the shingle. 'How long have you known I was following you?' she said, annoyed.

'Pretty much since you left The Crow,' said Salter. 'Cheer up. I'm glad you came out after me. I was beginnin to think I'd lost you in among all them troubled thoughts of yers.'

He smiled and Moss felt her crossness begin to fade.

'Come on,' he said. 'We can go along the shore a little if you like.'

They walked side by side in silence, until Salter finally said, 'So are you goin to tell me where you was that other night, or what?'

'I wanted to . . .' said Moss, 'but what I saw made me sick to my stomach. I just couldn't. After that, I don't know, you didn't seem interested.'

Salter opened his mouth as if to reply, then thought better of it. 'Is that what you was thinkin?' he said. 'Well, never mind, I'm interested now. All right then, out with it.'

It was a relief to tell him. It all spilled out, piece by piece. The whole horrible night at the Pit.

When she'd finished, at first Salter was at a loss to know how to respond.

'So let me get this straight. Yer tellin me you stayed half a night in a bear den? And then you saw animals from the Beast House fightin in a giant mud pit?'

'Yes,' said Moss.

'Where was this pit exactly?'

'Somewhere down the river. They called it The Dogs.'

'The *Isle of Dogs*?' Salter whistled. 'Rat's cheeks, Leatherboots! That ain't no place to go explorin, night or day or any time! It's all marsh an' swamp an' sinkin mud.'

'I was careful.'

'You was lucky.'

'Maybe . . .'

'An' who's this Whipmaster geezer then?'

'He's an Under-keeper in the Beast House. He takes animals from the Tower to the Pit. I saw him and his men take wolves that night.

'Well, there ain't nothin special about animal baitin. I ain't sayin I like it or nothin, just that there's bear baitin and cock fightin and all sorts goin on across the river all the time.'

'But it wasn't just animals in the ring, Salter, it was *people* too. There was a girl who sort of jumped over the wolves, and there was a man who had to fight them. They gave him a knife and a club.'

'You think they're baitin people against beasts in that mud pit?' said Salter frowning. 'There's some pretty nasty stuff goes on in this city, but I ain't never heard of *that*. And you say this keeper-man, Severs, he's the one who's controllin it all? And he works in the Beast House?'

'Yes.'

Salter shook his head. 'I never got why you wanted to go in that Beast House in the first place, let alone why you went back fer more.'

Moss hesitated. 'There was a little girl. The first day we went. A red-headed girl . . . I just wanted to see if she was there again.'

Salter laughed. 'Yer a bad liar, Leatherboots.'

A rich autumn sun parted the clouds. They'd walked a fair distance along the shore, past Belinsgate and the place where Salter's shack used to be. As they neared the Tower, Moss could see a crowd gathered on the wharf.

'Something's going on,' she said. 'Come on.' And she led Salter up the bank. As they squeezed through the crush of people, Moss could hear cries of delight. She and Salter popped out of the crowd at the front of the wharf.

It was the most extraordinary sight.

Looped around a timber post was a long iron chain. The chain dangled in the river, chinking against the side of the wharf. And on the other end of the chain was the great white bear.

'Salter! Look!'

'I'm lookin!'

They stared, transfixed, as the bear swam through the choppy water, trailing the iron chain from a collar on his neck.

About twenty yards out, he stopped and bobbed

in the waves. Then the white furry head disappeared under.

'Well, boil up me eyes,' said Salter in wonder.

After a few moments, the bear's head broke the surface and he rolled up on his back, holding a fat silver salmon in his paws.

'Ooooh,' breathed the crowd.

'He's fishing,' said Moss.

'*He?*'

'The girl I met said the white bear was a he.'

'Well, he or she, that bear knows what it's doin by the look of it,' said Salter. He shook his head. 'Ain't that a sight. A swimmin, fishin bear . . .'

They watched the white bear guzzle the salmon and dive back under the waves, his broad, flat back sinking gracefully. It seemed so unlikely, thought Moss. This enormous bear, weighed down with the thickest coat of fur, could swim like an otter.

Standing guard by the chain, just a few feet from where Moss and Salter stood, was one of the men from last night. The one they called Sully. He was nervous, watching the river, as though the bear might leap out at any moment and guzzle him too. But next to him were a handful of keepers with a burning brazier and iron rods at the ready. She saw one of them nudge Sully.

'Remember not to feed that tiger later.' He tapped the side of his nose. 'Wine not beer. Know what I mean?'

Sully nodded.

'An' don't let that bear go, whatever you do,' continued the keeper, 'or Severs will have yer teeth on a string around his neck.'

'I got him,' said Sully.

'Yer givin him too much slack! Tighten that chain or you'll never get him back. Here . . .' The keeper started yanking on the chain with Sully helping. The bear bobbed to the surface and the pair began jerking him towards the wharf.

Keeping their distance from the fishing bear were a few of the flat little boats used by the watermen to ferry their passengers from one side of the river to the other. Salter was chuckling at the watermen who were having a job holding them steady with all the excitement. In one of the boats sat an elegant lady with a small red-haired child. They were many yards out from shore, but Moss could see that the child was a girl and that she appeared to be waving. Was she waving at *her*? Now she was standing up in the boat and calling out. With a cry, Moss realised the girl was little Elizabeth. She stepped forward, about to wave back, but at that moment, the crowd shoved from behind.

One minute she was standing on the wharf. The next, she was falling.

It all happened so fast. The whoosh of air as she fell. Salter's yell from above. The shock of the freezing water as she hit the river.

The force of her fall took her down deep, the weight of her dress slowing her body to a stop. She didn't panic. The water was muddy green, but there was enough light to know which way was up. With a kick of her legs, she struck out for the surface.

A sudden swell carried her sideways, out into the river, away from the wharf. Her dress clung to her body, making her strokes more feeble than usual. She pulled hard with her arms, inching closer to the sparkling light above her.

Out of the murk came a white blur, tree-trunk paws strong against the current.

It was the bear.

Instinctively, Moss stopped swimming. Aware that she couldn't hold her breath for much longer, she made her body as still as she could while the bear swam towards her. She saw his hind legs splayed behind him like the rudder of a boat, while his powerful front paws swept through the water. His neck was stretched, his head above the surface. Had he seen her? There was no chance she could out-swim the creature to the wharf. All she could hope was that he had eaten his fill of fish and that, if he hadn't, he wouldn't mistake her for a salmon.

Then he dropped his head under the water. Motionless in the cold river, Moss found herself face to face with the great white bear, the improbable bulk of its body suspended before her, a huge sack of white fur rippling in the current.

There was nothing she could do. The bear was so close she could have reached out and touched him. His eyes were quizzical, drinking in this odd sight, staring at Moss for what seemed like forever. As she stared back, a strange excitement gripped her heart. It was as though she was in a dream. Anything could happen.

Then an arm grabbed her from above and her head broke the surface. Salter was spluttering next to her, dragging her back towards the wharf. A few kicks and they were there, Salter hooking his arm around one of the cross-timbers and pulling them both towards a wooden ladder fixed to the wharf wall. He was pushing her up the ladder now. Close to the top she felt many hands lift her up and out. Someone wrapped a cloak around her shoulders. Then Salter was by her side, steering her through the crowd, off the wharf and onto the shingle of the riverbank.

'You scared the life out of me, Leatherboots,' he said. 'For a minute there, I thought you was bear food.'

'It was the strangest thing. The bear swam right up and he just looked at me. For ages. I thought I must be dreaming.'

'Got to get you dry now,' said Salter rubbing her arms with the cloak.

Moss squeezed some water out of the hem of her dress and held out her hand to the autumn sun. 'If we sit here a while, the sun can dry us.'

'Hello,' said a bright voice behind them. On the bank, with her governess nowhere to be seen, stood Elizabeth.

Moss stood up quickly, pulling Salter and the cloak up with her. 'Hello,' she said.

'I saw you from the boat. I thought it was you! I'm sorry that you fell in the river.' Elizabeth beamed up at Moss.

'Where's your governess?' asked Moss, 'Are you hiding from her again?' Little Elizabeth was quite a handful. The governess seemed to have no control over her whatsoever. 'Won't she be worried about you?

'Champers, worried? But I always go back. *Je reviens toujours.* She's teaching me French! *And* Italian. And soon we'll be doing Flemish and Spanish too. Champers says the two most important things for a young lady are learning and honesty. Well, we do an awful lot of learning. And I try to be honest. I mean, I know I put a mouse in her hat this morning, but I absolutely told her that I'd done it afterwards.' Her berry-brown eyes flashed with mischief. 'Perhaps she didn't hear me. She *was* screaming quite loudly at the time.'

Moss laughed and the little Elizabeth burst out laughing too.

'I like you,' said Elizabeth suddenly. 'My name is Elizabeth. What is yours?'

'It's Moss.' Then remembering Salter was right beside her, she added, 'And this is my friend Salter.'

A shy 'Mornin' was all he could manage and

Salter's sudden awkwardness made Moss want to laugh all over again.

She drew the cloak tighter over her shoulders. 'I wondered whether you'd come back to see the white bear.'

'Well, I pestered and I pestered and in the end Champers gave in. She said perhaps it would take my mind off it.'

'Off what?'

'Off my father. I saw him you know. After the christening of my baby brother Edward.'

'Edward?' Suddenly Moss remembered who she was talking about. The baby *Prince* Edward. She'd heard talk in the tavern a few days back of the christening of the King's son, her ears pricking at the mention of Hampton Court Palace.

'It was a good day,' said the little girl. 'Lady B carried baby Edward all the way up the aisle of the chapel. And there were lords and ladies holding a golden canopy over him. And they let me carry the cloth to wipe his head and there were candles and torches and singing and the roof of the chapel was twinkling with stars.'

It was a picture beyond Moss's imagining. A royal christening. But it had made Elizabeth happy and Moss could see the pride on her face as she spoke of all the people who had watched her as she carried the cloth for her baby brother.

'Afterwards I saw my father. Of course, he didn't speak to me. But he was beaming at everyone. And Champers says that when the King is happy then all England should be happy, and when he is angry then all England had better watch out.'

'I think Champers is probably right.'

'I am not afraid of him, you know.' Elizabeth's eyes sparked and Moss saw the same determined expression she'd first noticed when the girl had faced the great white bear a few days before. 'One day he will speak to me. I know he will. And when he does, I will ask him.'

'Ask him what?'

'About my mother. No one will talk about her,

no one. Not even Champers.' She lowered her voice. 'But I know some things. I know her name was Anne. And I know my sister Mary thinks she fussed about her clothes and her furs when she should have been on her knees in prayer. But Mary thinks that anyone who doesn't spend at least ten hours a day praying to Almighty God, is as heathen as a Barbary pirate!'

Moss couldn't help smiling. But inside she was sad for this little girl, who had never known her mother and one day would have to make sense of the way she'd died. On Tower Green. A blink of an eye, a flash of a sword and her head in a basket.

Moss reached into the wet pocket of her dress. The silver bird was still there. She was about to bring it out, but the cry of the governess made her turn her head. When she looked back, Elizabeth had gone.

Salter whistled. 'Was that really . . .?'

Moss nodded. 'It's just so sad, Salter. She doesn't even know what happened to her mother. All she knows is that her name was Anne and that she died.'

'Well don't go feelin too sorry for her, Leatherboots. She ain't got such a bad life if she's learnin French with boat trips on the river and a nice posh lady to look after her.'

'Perhaps.' Moss felt the silver bird in her pocket, the prick of its sharp beak. It bothered her that this child might grow up hearing only cruel gossip about her mother. But what could she do? Maybe she should have given her the bird, told her a little about her mother even. But now that chance was gone. She shook her head. She had not come to London to chase a mischievous princess.

Moss pulled the wet cloth of her dress from her legs and splayed it in the sunshine. Up on the wharf, the crowd was dispersing and Moss could see the keepers herding the bear back up the path to the Tower.

Across the river, the breeze rippled the calm water. Somewhere out there, the Riverwitch was waiting. Either she must find a way to deliver the

Whipmaster, or the Witch would come for her. What did the Riverwitch want with Severs though? The Pit was a vile and savage thing, but why would the Riverwitch care what happened there? She remembered the Witch's blackened hand. *Something evil was stirring*, the Witch had told her. But what could it be? The answer, she suspected, lay in the Pit. And though the idea of going back to that awful place filled her with horror, that was exactly what she felt she must do.

CHAPTER FIFTEEN
Salter's Way

Moss sat on the shore, her dress crisping in the midday sun. Salter had disappeared a little while ago, but she could see him now, hurrying across the shingle towards her, waving a loaf of bread and a hunk of something that looked very much like cheese.

He sat down beside her and broke the bread and cheese in two. They ate ravenously, without saying a word, and Moss felt the warmth of a much-needed meal flood through her body.

'Ain't nothin like that fer a hungry gut,' said Salter. 'Where would we be without bread an' cheese, eh?'

Moss smiled. 'Nowhere,' she said. 'It's the best food there is.'

For a while they sat together and Moss found herself looking at Salter, at the mess of his hair, at the crinkle of his weatherworn face, at the restless hands that could make a boat from driftwood. She couldn't explain it. She wanted nothing more than Salter there beside her. Yet something also made her want to push him away.

'Salter . . .'

'Mmm?'

'I have to go back. To the Pit.'

'Sweet Mary's Carbuncles! What for?'

She couldn't tell him.

'What are you up to, Leatherboots? There's a whole cartload of stuff goin on in that head of yours, ain't there?' He faced her. 'I know yer up to something crazy.'

'I need your help.'

'Why?'

'To get into the Pit.'

'But why would you want to go back in there again?'

'I can't tell you.' There was no way he'd help her if he knew she was planning to sneak into the Pit to spy on the Whipmaster. Her ears had pricked on Tower Wharf when she'd heard the keepers teasing Sully about the tiger. She was sure that meant there was going to be a fight at the Pit that night. And she reckoned she'd worked out a way to get in without being seen.

'Will you help me or not?'

'*Not*,' said Salter emphatically. Then his face softened. 'Can't you just tell me why? Why all these secrets an' mad ideas an' what are we even *doin* here in the first place?'

She opened her mouth to reply and for a fleeting moment she was tempted to tell him about the Riverwitch, and just try and make him understand that however dangerous it was to go bargaining with a Witch, it was better than a life lived in fear.

Salter's eyes were searching hers. So much had changed between them since they had met that very first time. Back then he was full of suspicion. Defensive. Always looking out for himself. But slowly, gradually, as they'd got to know each other, their friendship had grown And Moss realised that just as her instinct was to try and protect him, he would do anything to protect her too. If she told him about the Riverwitch, he would try to stop her.

So instead, she heard herself saying, 'If you won't help me, I could always ask Eel-Eye Jack.'

'What? Fer goodness sakes, stop askin favours from that slippery-tongued cheater.'

'He's not a cheater, he's kind and –'

'He's as bent as a twisted stick, only yer too blind to see it.'

'Don't be ridiculous. Can't you just accept that Eel-Eye Jack is helping us because, I don't know, because he likes us or maybe he feels sorry for us? It's only *you* who thinks he's bad.'

'*Bad* don't go far enough for that scavvy dog-stealer!'

'They're strays, Salter, he doesn't steal them. And *scavvy*? That's not even a word.'

Salter shook his head. 'Don't get mixed up in his business. You don't know what he's up to.' There was a desperation in his voice that Moss hadn't heard before. 'An' don't think I don't know,' he said.

'Know what?'

'Don't think I didn't see you that night, climbin up on the roof at sunset.'

Moss felt herself redden under his gaze. He'd *seen* her?

'So what?' she said. 'What's wrong with that? Eel-Eye Jack was showing me something. The view. The clouds, they were like mountains, it was beautiful.'

'I'll bet.' Salter turned away, looking miserable.

'What is *wrong* with you?'

'Never mind.' He had his back to her and stayed like that for several minutes, shoulders hunched.

Moss stared out across the river. The water was

lapping the shore with a filthy-looking froth. As the waves drew back, they left fish lying on the shingle, brown and lifeless, as though they'd been dipped in mud. The waft of rotting meat drifted by.

What's goin on with this river?' said Salter at last. 'It ain't usually so bad as this.'

Soon, all will rot and turn to mud. The Riverwitch was right. The river was dying.

Moss stood up to climb the bank.

'Wait!'

Salter was at her side. 'Don't . . .' he said.

'I'm going, Salter.'

'All right then. I'll help you.'

'You will?'

Salter was staring at her, eyes wide-brown with something that looked almost like fear. 'If you got to go back to the Pit, I know a way' he said. 'But I'm comin with you.'

A wave of relief swept through Moss. She looked at her friend and wanted to smile, but the smile would not come.

It was dusk and Moss was waiting at the end of the alley. Salter had told her to meet him there and she wished he'd hurry up. If there was to be a fight tonight in the Pit, she was guessing the keepers would be taking the tiger by boat, just as before. But Salter wasn't planning on sneaking on to the boat at all. He said he'd get them to the Pit his own way. Then he'd vanished, leaving her to finish her stew in The Crow.

'Come on,' she muttered, hopping from one foot to another. There was a chill in the air and the dark alley was not the most welcoming place to hang about.

A trundle of wheels over cobbles snapped her to attention. Around the corner came a small cart and donkey, with a squat man at the reins and Salter sitting next to him.

The cart stopped next to Moss and Salter jumped down.

'Yer carriage, m'lady!' he grinned and gestured

to the cart, which appeared to be filled with lumpy sacks. 'Mr Jibby here is goin our way with the turnips he couldn't sell at market an' fer a small price he'll carry us to The Dogs. Hop in!'

Moss scrambled on and nestled herself between the turnip sacks, Salter beside her. With a flick of the reins, Mr Jibby urged on his donkey and the cart rolled out of the alley.

It was a fine way to see the city, thought Moss, as the cart trundled through Cheapside, along the long, wide street Salter called Leadenhall, past spindle-spired churches and glass windows that twinkled with candles. Eventually they came to the city wall. The toll men waved Mr Jibby through and they set off up a winding hill.

'Say goodbye to the city,' said Salter. 'We're in lawless country now.'

'What do they call this place?' said Moss.

'Stepney,' said Salter.

All Moss could see was dirt track with fields either side.

'It's a no man's land out here,' said Salter, 'Robbers and all sorts. See old Jibby there? One hand on the reins? You can bet yer earlobes, his other hand's restin on his club. Any robber tries his luck with Mr Jibby an' he'll wake up on the path next mornin with a lump on his head the size of Christmas.'

Moss kept a sharp eye out after that, but soon they met a trickle of other people, some in carts, some on horseback, most on foot, all heading in the same direction.

'Wooahh there!' called Mr Jibby and the cart came to a stop. 'This is as close as I'm goin to the Isle of Dogs.'

'Right you are,' said Salter, and he and Moss jumped down.

'Just follow them people now,' said Mr Jibby. 'Can't say I likes the sound of what's goin on down there, but if that's where yer headin, good luck to yer.'

The trickle became a crowd, jostling its way down a narrow track. Before them stretched the Isle of Dogs, a huge curl of marshland that stuck out into the river like a tongue. As they walked, Moss noticed the path was raised, a ridgeway several feet above the treacherous mud.

'What's the plan then?' asked Salter. 'Got a groat to get us in if we need it.'

A groat? Where had he got that kind of money from? But she didn't want to get into an argument. Right now she had to focus. She needed to get close to Severs. To find out what he was up to and work out a way to bring him to the river.

In the distance she could just make out the high basin-shaped walls of the Pit.

'There it is.' She tugged Salter's arm.

The night was still, carrying the shouts of men and the bark of dogs over the marsh. As they drew nearer, the crush of people jostling to get through the gates drove them forwards.

'Hey!' Salter shoved a man to his left, who shoved back, pushing him into the path of another man, who lifted Salter by the scruff of his neck and shouted in his face before putting him down.

'Watch where yer goin, boy!' Moss could smell beer on the man's sour breath.

She dragged Salter to one side, out of the path of the surging crowd.

'This place is horrible,' said Salter, 'Remind me what we're doin here?'

But Moss didn't reply. She'd seen something. To the right of the Pit, across the mud to the shore, a boat was landing. A boat she recognised.

'Quick! Salter! This way!' She scrambled down the side of the pathway into the mud. Dodging between old crates and cast-off timbers and sticking to whatever shadows she could find, she made her way around the curve of the Pit wall. A cart was already rattling over the slats of the wooden bridge.

They stopped a few yards from the back gate.

'What are we doin here?' whispered Salter, 'Why don't we just go in the front door?'

'I don't want to go in through the front,' said

Moss. 'I want to find out more about this place. I need to get in through the back.'

'Eh?'

'Look, I need you to draw the attention of those men away from the cart for just a few seconds. That's all I need.'

'All you need to do what?'

'Never mind that,' said Moss. If she was right, on board that cart was a sleeping tiger. She'd tuck herself in next to it, just like last time. And when she was through the gate, she'd find a good moment to crawl out.

'I don't like it,' said Salter. 'Let's go back round the front. Pay our way in.'

'No, wait! Please! Salter, come on! Just do this one thing for me! It's . . . important.'

Salter hesitated.

The cart was nearly at the gate. It was trundling to a halt.

'Now!' said Moss, shoving Salter out into the mud and scurrying forward, tucking herself behind a timber support just a few feet from the gate. She turned to see Salter staggering about in the mud, waving his arms.

'Oi oi!' he shouted to the men. Then he began to sing.

> *Here's a health to the barley mow, my brave boys!*
> *Here's a health to the barley mow!*
> *We'll drink it out of the jolly brown bowl*
> *Here's a health to the barley mow!*

While he sang, he swayed towards the men, pitching forward and wandering back, as though he was drunk. Moss almost laughed with delight at his performance. And it was doing the trick too, for all the men had turned to watch the drunken boy singing a harvest song in the mud.

This was her chance. While the men jeered at Salter, she crept forward and climbed on to the back of the cart, tucking herself quickly under the oilcloth.

It was dark and the air was choked with the musk of an enormous animal. She could just about make out a vague pattern of stripes running across its back. It was the tiger. Thankfully it was fast asleep.

We'll drink it out of the quarter pint, my brave boys!
Here's a health to the barley mow!
We'll drink it out of the jolly brown bowl
The quarter pint, the nipperkin and the jolly brown
  bowl
Here's a health to the barley mow!

She heard Salter finish his song, followed by cheers and insults from the men. Then came a shout to the gate.

'Open up! Open up!'

In front of them, the gate creaked open. The cart was moving. She felt it trundle in and jerk to a stop.

'Leave it now, Sully! That beast won't be wakin just yet. Better see to the dogs first.'

Now there was silence.

As gently as she could, Moss lifted the edge of the oilcloth. There was a torch burning on the wall of what looked an earth room. It smelled of mud and damp. At one end was a hefty wooden door, at the other end a smaller gate. The only sound was the slow breathing of the sleeping tiger and her own heart thudding deep inside her chest.

She was alone.

Quickly, noiselessly, Moss whipped back the oilcloth and swung herself off the cart. As her feet touched the soft earth floor, something darted across the edge of her eyeline. A flash of red. Before she could even cry out, cold metal pressed against the flesh on her neck.

A silver blade, glinting in the torchlight.

Then a voice, soft in her ear.

'Move and I'll cut yer throat.'

CHAPTER SIXTEEN
Jenny Wren

The blade stayed where it was, pressed to the hollow in Moss's neck. Her head was yanked back, sinews stretched tight, and she could not see the hand that held it. She tried to peer down and felt the flat metal push harder.

'I *said*, move and I'll cut yer throat.'

Slowly, from behind her, an arm came to into view, followed by the head and shoulders of a young girl. She circled, like an animal ready to pounce, all the while keeping her blade at Moss's throat. She wore a rust-red tunic of beaten leather, belted at the waist. Her dirt-brown breeches were like a boy's and her black hair was woven into two plaits. It was the girl from the ring. The one who'd run and leapt with the wolves. Up close, Moss could see that the tattered scarf around her head was scarlet silk, flecked with gold daggers.

'What you doin here?'

Moss swallowed. 'Take that knife away and I'll tell you.'

The girl's eyes flashed. She stretched out her other hand and patted Moss's dress on one side, all the way from her shoulders to her knees. When she got to Moss's pocket, she stopped and slipped her hand inside, pulling out the silver bird.

'Ow!' She dropped the bird and in an instant, Moss had batted the knife away, but the girl was quicker and darted in front of Moss before she could take so much as a step.

Now the knife was to Moss's chest. With a jab of her boot, the girl flicked the silver bird up from the floor, catching it in her other hand, her eyes still trained on Moss.

'I'll ask again,' said the girl, 'What you doin here?'

Moss knew she didn't have much time. The keepers could be back at any moment. 'My name is Moss . . .' *Don't give too much away*, she thought. 'I came from a village. I came looking for . . . the one they call the Whipmaster.'

'Severs? What you want with him?'

'He . . . he . . .' *Quick, think.* 'I know someone. She wants to meet the Whipmaster. But . . . he mustn't know who she is.'

The girl's eyes narrowed. 'Why mustn't he know?'

'He will not meet her if he does.'

'Why not?'

'He's afraid of her.'

'Severs? Afraid?' The girl chuckled bitterly. 'He ain't afraid of nuthin nor no one.'

Moss remembered the savage kick from Severs' boot that had sent the girl tumbling back into the ring.

'He's lord and king of the Isle of Dogs,' the girl went on, 'He rules this place with fear and fire. And there ain't a man nor beast can make him tremble.' Then her face lit up with the eagerness of a sudden thought. 'I'll tell you somethin though. I'd give anythin to see him cowerin an' cryin like them poor beggars in the ring. If you can make Severs afraid, maybe I won't cut yer throat after all.'

She lowered the blade and Moss felt her neck relax.

'I saw you,' said Moss. 'In the ring. With the wolves. *Jenny Wren.*'

'That's right,' said the girl. 'Been here before then?'

'I climbed the earth wall. I looked over the top. I saw you leaping and springing, and when you jumped up on the wolf's head I thought you were flying.'

'Stayin alive is what I'm doin.'

'But don't you ever get hurt?'

'Nah, I'm too good.' The girl's face burned

fierce in the torchlight. 'One day I'll get out of here though.'

'You're a prisoner?'

'*He* keeps me here. I'm his star attraction, see? The ones that come here, they ain't never seen nuthin like me.' She shook her head. 'Severs won't let me go. He says the only way I'm gettin out is feet first, dragged off with the dead dogs.'

'What about the other fighters? I saw a man with a knife and club that night, in the ring with the wolves. After you.'

'With them ones it's fifty-fifty. Depends what they're up against. That one who fought the wolves, he lived, but he ain't good for another fight, so he'd have been sent packin. But the ones that don't make it, they gets dragged out and dumped in the marsh –' She stopped, tensing at the sound of voices. 'Quick! They're comin!' With a flick of her hand, she tossed the silver bird back to Moss. 'Take yer little knife and get under there!' She pushed Moss to the floor and rolled her under a low bench, throwing over a sack and sitting down hard, just as a wicker gate creaked open.

'Time to go, Little Wren.'

Moss heard the rustling of the oilcloth and the sound of men straining to lift the tiger from the cart. One of them whistled.

'Sweet Devil's Lungs! Look at the teeth on that! They call this a *tiger*. You ever danced with a tiger, Little Wren? Heh heh!'

The room filled with coarse laughter.

'Don't laugh too loud,' said the girl. 'I heard tigers ain't got a sense of humour. I heard the last one that got woken by a bunch of fat, dirty men laughin their stinkin breath in its face, that tiger ripped off its bindins and bit out their throats. An' then they couldn't laugh no more.'

'Don't listen to her,' said one of the men. But there were no more jokes after that and they dragged the tiger out of the room in silence.

They were gone. Moss was alone.

Now what? It was Severs she needed to get close

to. But how could she do that? She looked down at her green dress. She'd stand out a mile among the jeering, shouting men on the terraces. There was no chance of blending in while she was wearing a dress. She looked around the room. In one corner, there was a little pile of clothes. They must belong to Jenny, thought Moss. She picked them up. There were breeches worn to the knees, a rough linen shirt and a faded red leather tunic. Could she just borrow them? Somehow she doubted she'd get a chance to give them back, but what could she do?

Moss pulled the breeches up and tucked her dress inside them. The linen shirt she dragged over her head followed by the leather tunic, which she smoothed down as best she could. Among the clothes were lengths of torn cloth and Moss tied one of these round her head, bundling her tangled hair underneath. She was an odd-looking sort of boy, but in the dark and feverish atmosphere of the Pit, she hoped no one would notice.

Moss crept across the room to the wicker gate

and peered through the woven slats. A wide open-roofed passage led from the room, just a channel of earth shored up wth timbers. The glow of torches at its end told her that this was most likely the way to the ring. The roar was getting louder, mixed with the unmistakable snarl of fighting dogs.

The passage was empty, but now that she looked more closely, Moss saw ladders which she guessed climbed to the terraces. Pressing herself flat to the wall on one side, she made her way along until she reached one. She climbed cautiously, up and up, peeping to make sure her guess was right. Then she scrambled over the top, finding herself at once among the mash of bodies on the terraces. She made her way behind them, tripping over chicken bones and cockleshells and gagging on the fug of beery breath that hung in the air.

'BEASTS! BEASTS! BEASTS!' The yells were all around her. Moss covered her ears and looked about. Severs was on his throne on the terrace opposite. She was about to make her way round the terrace, when the cry went up for the girl.

'JEN-NY WREN! JEN-NY WREN!'

There she was, balancing on the lip of the terrace. Her mask was on, but Moss could see her eyes darting this way and that.

Below her, the tiger was on its feet, the stripes above its eyes twitching. Its powerful body was fur and muscle, a rippling bulk of orange, striped with white and black. It walked slowly, almost lazily, the ridge of its back swaying with the careful pad of one huge paw in front of another. There was a fearlessness about the tiger. It would not give way to the taunts of the men, thought Moss.

'JEN-NY WREN! JEN-NY WREN!'

The girl threw her head back to the gaping sky above the Pit, as though she was taking a last breath. Then she leapt, plunging into the arena. And with a single bound of its powerful paws, the tiger was upon her.

Moss clamped her hand to her mouth. The arena was a blur of orange-black fur as the tiger sprang, front and hind legs outstretched, the white of its underbelly streaking towards Jenny Wren. Jenny rolled and leapt to her feet as the tiger's great paws came crashing down, inches from her shoulder. She sprinted up the side of the earth bowl, towards the very place where Moss crouched. But just as Jenny's hands clawed at the lip of the bowl she slipped. Below her, the tiger pounced, jaws snapping at her heels.

It was a split-second thing. As the tiger coiled to spring again, Moss's eyes met Jenny Wren's and she saw panic and terror and the look of someone who could taste her own death. Without thinking, Moss swiped a burning torch from its bracket and shoved it into Jenny's hand. Just as the tiger leapt up the wall, the girl thrust the flames at the creature's face. It bit down hard, its jaws clamping like a trap around the torch and dragging it back down to the ground. The tiger shook the flames until they were beaten to smoke on the earth floor.

The crowd went crazy – a screaming, jumping

frenzy – drunk on the closeness of death and the fire-quenching tiger.

From his throne of animal skins, Severs cracked his whip, signalling the end of Jenny's bout. Moss shrank back, trying to hide herself among the jostling bodies. She hadn't meant to attract attention to herself. Now she must hide until everyone was distracted by something else.

Burying herself in the crush of legs, she pushed and crawled her way around the terrace, popping out in the row behind the throne of skins. She eased herself nearer, as close as she dared, close enough to hear the jagged words of the Whipmaster to the men either side of him. She would wait and she would watch. Pick up anything she could. And when the fight was finished, she would follow him.

That was her plan.

She couldn't believe she had got this far.

CHAPTER SEVENTEEN
Slider

'We'll be runnin out of dogs at this rate. That's twenty down so far, Severs.'

'Who's counting? Can't you see their faces. They've never seen a spectacle like this.'

'I'm only sayin, that tiger's makin short work of em.'

'Then better make sure you got enough in supply, eh, Fagg? That's what I pay you for. Or would you rather I went elsewhere for fighting dogs?'

'Ain't no one breeds fightin dogs like John Fagg.

And none that'll sell to you without the say-so from me. Cut me out an yer whole Pit crumbles, Severs.'

'Is that right?' Moss could hear the bristle in the Whipmaster's voice. She crept a little closer, still peeping through the forest of legs.

With a sudden jerk, Severs grabbed the man's hand and pinned it flat to the armrest of his throne. He held a knife, poised above Fagg's little finger.

'You like fingers, Fagg?'

'I –'

'*I* like fingers, Fagg. And the thing I like most is we've got so many of them. You wouldn't think a man would notice if he lost one, now, would you?'

Moss watched Fagg, his body rigid, his eyes locked on the knife. The only thing moving was the vein pulsing in his neck.

Severs let go of his hand and watched the man rub his throbbing wrist.

'Now, what were you saying, John Fagg? Will I have the dogs I need?'

'Yes.'

'Good. Always nice to know where you stand in business.' Severs gestured quickly to the arena and a smile cut his face. 'Ever wondered what we do with all the dead ones?'

The man shook his head.

'Well I've got a hankering to show you. So don't go running off after the show. You'll be by the side gate, where they drag the dogs out.'

At that moment the arena exploded with an ear-splitting roar and Severs stood up, pushing Fagg aside. She saw him disappear from the terrace and the crowd fell into a sudden silence, all eyes on the arena. On one side the snarling tiger paced, its paw hanging ragged. Twenty men had it surrounded, jabbing with torches and hot irons to hold it back. In the middle of the ring, curled in the mud was the lifeless body of a man. Striding towards him was Severs.

All around Moss the crowd began to chant.

'WHIPMASTER! WHIPMASTER!'

Severs took the whip from his thick leather belt,

bent down and lifted the man's head by his hair before letting it drop back to the ground. He rose, a look of satisfaction on his face. Unfurling the whip, he raised his arm and cracked it into the night sky.

The crowd erupted, their gutteral cries ripping through the arena. Tonight they had got what they came for and the sight of it was so sickening that Moss thought she might pass out.

She breathed deeply, heaving herself up. The show was over now and everyone began pushing along the terrace. Moss felt herself swept along by the crush, all the while trying to keep one eye on Severs who was disappearing through a door on the edge of the arena. Was that the way to the side gate? Soon the crowd were out through the main gates on open marsh, making their way back along the raised track to the road.

Moss slipped from the path and crouched in the shadow of the Pit. She needed to find that side gate. So she pressed her body to the wall and crept around, taking care to stay in the shadows. The noise of the crowd was fading now. Stretching in front of her was open marsh, lit by a low moon. She could hear voices and, as she eased herself further round the wall, she saw Severs' men dragging dog after dog through the gates, dumping them on a large wooden board. In the darkness she saw them carry another, larger body and flop it on to the pile.

'That's the last, Mr Severs.'

She watched the Whipmaster walk from the Pit with John Fagg following.

There was a strange silence among the men as Severs picked out three or four to take up the ropes of the board. The rest scuttled back inside the gates and Moss guessed that wherever it was the chosen few were going, the others were glad to stay behind.

The Whipmaster strode ahead and she watched the men heave on the ropes, dragging their cargo away from the Pit out on to the vastness of open marsh. The men trod carefully, sticking to a rigid line behind Severs, the suck of mud on their boots puncturing the still air.

When the men had made a good distance, Moss set off after them. She was careful to stick to the hummocks, skirting wide around the marshgrass, for she could see that it was treacherous. Long stems disappeared into pools that were still and black and looked deep enough to swallow the moon.

Up ahead, she could see the men had stopped. She slowed, heading for a muddy hummock and when she got there she crawled on to her belly and peeked over the top.

The men were just a few feet away, standing with their backs to her. They appeared to be huddled around some sort of hole in the ground and they'd covered their mouths and noses with their sleeves. At first Moss wondered why, then across the mud came a stench. A stench that made her eyes water and her stomach heave. Of things rotting. Of things that smelt as though they should have been buried or burned a long time ago.

She saw Severs kneel and flop a large bundle

into the hole. The men passed him another and another until Moss counted seven bundles tipped into the hole.

He was talking. Low words, growled like a bitter prayer. Sinking into the deep quiet of the marsh.

One to open marshland deep
One for bones of men asleep
One for blood in battle shed
One for a beast without a head
One to turn them all to mud
One to lift the dark's bent hood
One for the chaos that will rise
For none can stop the Slider

He rose to his feet. 'Throw in the rest.'

Moss saw fear clutch the faces of the men. None of them moved.

'Do it,' said the Whipmaster, 'unless you want to join them.'

Reluctantly the men began dragging the bundles

from the board. Moss watched them throw one after another into the hole, a long, deep drop to the bottom, where the faint squelch of muddy water answered back.

While they worked, Severs hauled one man roughly to his side.

'Look down, Fagg.'

'What . . . what is it?'

'See the darkness? Ancient darkness. It guards its treasure. Bricks and bones and the bodies of men. But there's more than just darkness deep down in the mud.'

'What is down there?'

The moonlight caught Severs' flint stare. But before he could reply, Moss felt the ground move beneath her feet.

'The one I have woken grows stronger now,' rasped the Whipmaster. 'Listen. It stirs.'

Something was moving in the mud. Something long and thick and dark. A rolling shape. A rise and fall like a slow wave.

It disappeared. A few feet away it rose again, then again nearby.

The men held on to each other in terror.

'Stay where you are!' ordered Severs.

From deep inside the hole, there was a swish followed by the sucking of mud and a frenzied slapping, as though something was beating its body against the sides.

'More!' cried Severs. 'Throw the rest in!'

The trembling men kicked more bundles into the hole. Again, Moss heard the frenzied beating against the deep walls.

The sight of whatever was down there was too much for Fagg. With a sudden jerk of his arm, he pulled away from Severs and ran.

Moss let out a little gasp. He was running straight for her. And the eyes of every man turned to where she was crouching.

She ducked behind the hummock. Had they seen her? What would they do if they caught her? Take her back to the Pit? Make her fight beasts like

Jenny Wren? Or throw her down that hole to face whatever lurked at the bottom?

There was nowhere to go. All around was wide open marsh with too many yards between her and the next mound of mud. She was trapped.

In front of her, hidden from the view of the men, was a clump of tall stems rising from the dark-water pool. Quick as she could, Moss scrabbled towards the grass and, with no time to change her mind, dropped down into the black water.

The pool wasn't deep at all. Tepid and still, the water only just reached her shoulders. Beneath her feet, soft mud shifted, squirming between her toes, and Moss wished for the cold, clean river back home. But none of that mattered because from behind the hummock came the shouts of men. The marsh pool was dark and she did her best to tuck herself among the slender stems, but Moss knew her white face would be lit by the moon for all to see. She would have to hold her breath under the water for as long as she could. She was about to take a great lungful of air, when a thought snapped into her head. The marshgrass! She ripped a stem from the mud, broke off the end and put it to her lips. It was hollow. Lowering her head and shoulders under the water, Moss tilted her head back, taking care to leave the end of the stem poking above the surface. The fetid water stung her eyes. But she could breathe.

Winding her other arm around the submerged grass, she anchored herself to the mud bed, trying to keep her body as still as possible. The shouts of men were close now. She could hear them as they came tumbling over the hummock. And from her watery hiding place she saw the legs of Fagg buckle right beside the pool, saw the others haul him up in front of Severs. She watched as Severs spoke to him. Then the men dragged him to his feet and they were gone.

Slowly, Moss lifted her head from the pool and spat the stem from her mouth. She stood up and squinted into the darkness of the marsh. The men were making their way back to the Pit. Digging her hands into the muddy sides of the pool, she heaved her body up. Getting out was not as easy as she'd thought. Her hands and knees slipped in the sludge and she dropped back into the water. She was about to try again, when something brushed her leg. Instinctively she flinched. A fish? Surely no fish could live in this rancid pool. She scanned the murky surface, but the water was so choked, she could see nothing.

There it was again. Something solid sliding past her leg. She kicked out under the water and a few feet away, the surface of the pool broke with a flick of something black and glistening. A shadowy, muscular trunk, arcing in the water.

Moss had never moved so fast. She threw herself at the mud, launching one leg halfway up the bank, kicking and clawing her way out and when she'd scrambled clear, she turned, panting on all fours, to see what was there.

For a few seconds, the oil-black water bubbled before settling back to a rippling pool.

She scrabbled away from the edge. Salter had warned her about sinking mud that would suck a person down without a trace. But this was more than sinking mud. There was something down there. Some *thing*.

The Whipmaster's words crawled inside her head, spider's feet that probed and pricked. Their meaning was there, but she could not quite grasp it.

> *One to turn them all to mud*
> *One to lift the dark's bent hood*
> *One for the chaos that will rise*

The thing Severs had woken. The ancient, evil thing that lurked and slithered and slapped in the mud. The name snagged her throat. It made her sick with fear. To go near the Whipmaster was to go near that thing.

The Slider.

CHAPTER EIGHTEEN
The River Inside

Moss knew it would take her the rest of the night to walk back to London from the Isle of Dogs. She began by following the river, although it did not feel like the river she knew. The water here was a stagnant stew that slopped against the shore. A mile up river from the Isle and she could still feel the reach of that creature. Everywhere was mud, pulling and sucking at her ankles just as it had in the marsh. The shoreline was littered with gaping fish and rotting eels and lifeless birds with crooked necks, their bodies slick with mud. It was as the Riverwitch had said: the river was suffocating. The power of the Slider was growing.

She never thought the Tower would be a welcome sight, but when it finally came into view, Moss found herself hurrying towards it, a beacon, guiding her back to the city. By the time she reached Tower Wharf, dawn was breaking. Here the river was its usual grey-green murk with the smell of salt and seaweed all around. She peeled off her clothes, leaving just Jenny Wren's long white shirt to cover herself with and washed each garment as best she could in the shallows. The woollen dress came up almost as clean as the day Pa had given it to her and the sight of it brightened her heart.

Next she waded in to scrub the mud-stench from her skin. Waist-deep she stood, rubbing her face and arms with a fistful of dry bladderwrack and when the seaweed had scoured her body, she dived under the chop of a wave, letting it pull at her hair. The grey water was cold and Moss forced her arms into quick, strong strokes to touch the river bed, kicking off again to burst to the surface.

It was low tide, and though there was an urgency to the drift of the current, it was not the furious pull and suck that had near-drowned her so many times. Moss forgot the cold and dived down, opening her eyes. She let the current carry her a little way down river, rising to take a breath, then dropping below the surface.

In the flow of water a dark shape was floating towards her. A shape she knew only too well.

River Daughter . . .

Moss froze. She wanted to swim away, but now the current picked up speed, sweeping her into the Riverwitch's cold embrace. Her breath was gone, yet she was not choking. She clung on, her hands grasping at the gossamer tendrils of cloth and weed. The creeping rot had spread along the bone-thin arms, blackening them to their roots.

The tattered face of the Witch stared down at Moss.

'The rot spreads. It creeps. Water will turn to

mud. River after river will dry and crack. The wells will empty, the crops will wither. I am the river. Without me, all will die.'

Moss felt her veins run cold, as though the icy water mixed with her blood. As though the river was inside her. As though it *was* her.

'You must keep your bargain. Bring him. Bring the one who feeds it to me.'

'But I can't.' Moss heard her own voice, echoing in the water. 'He's got men all around him all the time. And . . . that beast in the mud. It's impossible.'

'There is a way . . .'

The Witch's bone fingers tightened on hers.

'You must kill him.'

'What? No! I –'

Moss felt the Witch's grasp slacken. All around them, the water swirled and the Riverwitch glided back, into the drift of the current. Moss watched the billowing fronds of her garments float upwards, as if blown by a wind. The Witch's voice carried with them.

'Find a way . . . to kill him.'

Moss burst from the water and struggled back to shore. She lay on the shingle panting, the breath returning to her lungs. She must have been under for minutes. Wrapped in the Witch's embrace, she'd breathed the river as though it was fresh air. She could feel its cool fingers, even now, on the shore, she could feel it holding her, carrying her, she could feel herself diving down into the bottomless river, a river that flowed right through her.

But the river was dying. She'd seen with her own eyes – the rotting fish and birds. She'd smelt the stench. What if the words of the Riverwitch were true? What if the people died with it?

Behind her, from the Tower, came a roar that shook her bones, for she knew it was the great white bear. Trapped. Confused. Part of the Whipmaster's terrifying world. Of beast-fights and death and creatures that rose from the mud. And Moss could see how a man like that could thrive in the chaos of a land spiralling to hell.

But to kill him . . . how could she even attempt such a thing?

Moss pushed open the door and walked into The Crow. In the shuttered half-light, a few people lay slumped in chairs, sleeping off the night. She padded towards the fireplace and knelt as close as she could, holding her palms to the crackling logs. The warmth was good.

She'd only been there for a few moments when she felt the weight of a blanket placed on her shoulders. Strong arms wrapped it around her and she turned, expecting to see Salter.

'A girl this cold should have a warm blanket.'

Her heart jumped.

Eel-Eye Jack drew the blanket gently across her collarbone.

'You are frozen like the mountain snow, Moss-from-the-village.'

He sat down next to her and rested his elbows

on his knees. In the firelight his face was open, searching hers.

'A girl should not have such disregard for herself.'

She pulled the blanket tighter. Underneath, her dress was still wet, but she realised she'd stopped shivering.

'This is not my business,' said Eel-Eye Jack, 'but you, out alone all the night? It is not wise or safe.'

'I know,' said Moss.

Eel-Eye Jack reached out and peeled a lock of wet hair from Moss's cheek. His fingers brushed her skin as he pushed it back amongst the tangle behind her ears. Moss felt a rush of heat, then guilt for feeling it and anger at Salter for not being there. Where *was* he?

Eel-Eye Jack was looking at her with an intensity that made her want to look away. But she didn't.

'An adventurous spirit will carry you far from home,' he said. 'Show you the world's wonders and

243

its horrors. But the moment we forget . . . forget our home, forget ourselves, then we are lost.'

The logs on the fire crackled and spat.

'Are you lost?' he said.

Moss shook her head. But she *was* lost. Far from home. Far from Pa. What was she doing here?

His blue-flame eyes held hers. 'Tell me, did you find the one you sought?'

She nodded.

'So you have done what you came for?'

Moss was silent.

'I have given you food and a roof. And now I ask for something in return.'

Moss drew the blanket tight. 'What?'

'Go home. Leave this place. Go back to your village.'

'Are we a burden to you? If we are, then perhaps I could work for you? Earn our keep?'

'The work I do is not for you.'

Moss stared at him, trying to look beyond the cool burn of his gaze. There were shadows there.

Hiding. Cast by the glowing fire, she saw them creep across his brow. But she did not know what they meant.

'Please. I can't go back yet.'

Eel-Eye Jack ran a hand through his sand-blond hair.

'When you look at me, what do you see? What am I?'

'You are . . . I don't know. You are the music that comes from you.'

'The music is in me,' said Eel-Eye Jack. 'But it is not *me*.'

'I see the places in your head, faraway thoughts,' said Moss, 'and kindness. You have been good to us, to me and Salter.'

Eel-Eye Jack looked into the fire and for a moment she thought she could see brightness among the shadows on his face. Whatever was troubling him, perhaps there was a way out of it?

'Jackin . . .' she said softly.

He reached out a hand and with his fingertips

gently touched her cheek.

'You have chased a little of my darkness away, Moss-from-the-village. It has been a long time since I have felt such a kindred spirit. In another life, perhaps –'

'*Perhaps what?*'

Salter's voice cut through the stillness of the tavern. He stood in the doorway, misery and disbelief all over his face.

'Salter!' Moss jumped up and the blanket dropped to the floor. Eel-Eye Jack picked it up and placed it back around her shoulders.

'Nice an' cosy is it? The two of you, by the fire?' Salter's words faltered a little, as though he could not quite bring himself to say them. 'Am I interruptin somethin?'

'No! Don't be ridiculous. Come and get warm too.' Moss took a step towards him. But Salter was glaring at Eel-Eye Jack.

'Stay away from her. I know what you are.'

'Do you?' Eel-Eye Jack stood facing Salter calmly.

'And you would judge me? You who have stolen and cheated?'

Salter looked as though he might explode. He scowled furiously as Eel-Eye Jack pulled open the door of the tavern then looked back at Moss.

'Are you a little warmer now?' said Eel-Eye Jack.

'Thank you. I am,' replied Moss.

She watched him walk through the door, a hundred questions burning in her head.

CHAPTER NINETEEN
Friendship Broken

'Well, thanks a lot for making such a spectacle of *nothing*,' said Moss when Eel-Eye Jack had gone.

'He was at the Pit,' said Salter.

'What? Who was at the Pit?'

'Fiddle-boy there. I heard the guards on the back gate talkin about him. After you'd gone in on that cart.'

'Oh, really? And what exactly did you hear?'

'Heard them say the name Jack. Talked about

him bein late an' where was his boat an' stuff. Said he should have been there hours ago with the prisoner.'

'And did you *see* Eel-Eye Jack?'

'No –'

'And were they talking about *Eel-Eye* Jack or just someone called Jack?'

'Just Jack, but –'

'Honestly, Salter! Do you have *any* idea how many people there are in this city who go by that name?'

'It was Eel-Eye. I felt it in me bones. Sure as old Henry's rotten leg.'

Moss was shaking her head. 'You're just angry. You'll say anything to make me think badly of him.'

'*What?*' Salter almost stamped his foot in exasperation. 'Why won't you listen to me? Anyway, that wasn't all them guards said. All right, it was just a word, but it ain't a word you hear every day.'

'What word?'

Salter frowned.

'Newgate.'

'Newgate?'

'Come on.' He grabbed her hand.

'Where are we going?'

'I've got a feelin I know what he's up to.'

Before Moss could object, Salter bustled her out of the inn and practically marched her down the alley.

They made their way up Cheapside, where the street was already buzzing. Hawkers and shopkeepers were banging open their doors, setting out their wares, calling to the people who were trickling into the street. Soon they found themselves in a narrow lane. Bobbling above Moss's head were dozens of paper-thin balls, milky-white and tethered to ropes stretched tight between the buildings.

'Bladder Street,' said Salter, nodding at a man with puffed cheeks who was blowing into a slippery object clasped between his palms. And Moss realised she'd seen men and women back in the village do the very same, blowing up the bladders of pigs and sheep, then hanging them out to dry for waterskins.

'Is this what you dragged me out here to see?'

Salter shook his head. 'Not there yet. Come on.'

He led her on through a street that reeked with the salt-iron smell of meat, where butchers chopped at fresh-slaughtered sheep and the gutter ran thick with blood. Moss covered her nose with her sleeve. She'd watched Mrs Bailey wring the necks of chickens and had once seen the farmer kill a pig, but here was a whole street of men and women whose job it was to slaughter animals all day long. In London, thought Moss, you could be among silk merchants one minute and carcasses the next. Life crowded these alleys and sucked you in and the best you could hope was that it wouldn't spit you out again.

As they left the butchers' lane, they passed a market house that rang with the cries of grain-sellers. Then the street widened and she realised Salter was looking all about, herding her towards the grain-sheds and telling her to keep herself tucked in amongst them and to stay behind him. Once or twice he stopped, peeking cautiously before they carried on. He was following someone. She was sure of it.

'Nearly there.'

'Salter –'

And then she caught sight of a shock of sand-blond hair ahead of them, weaving its way through the crowd.

'Oh, for goodness sake, I don't believe this.'

'What?' He pulled her after him.

'Stop, will you?'

'Come on!'

'No!' She grabbed his arm with both hands and jerked him to a halt, forcing him to face her. 'You're spying on him, aren't you? You're spying on Eel-Eye Jack. Sneaking around the streets and following him God knows where, hoping you'll catch him doing stuff that'll make him look bad. Stuff that you used to do *all the time*, Salter. Honestly, it's pathetic, it's –'

'Look,' said Salter pointing. Ahead of them was an enormous building. Windowless walls of grey stone rose like a fortress above the rickety market sheds.

'What's that?' asked Moss.

'That,' said Salter, 'is Newgate Prison.'

He tugged her hand. 'Come on.'

He led her past the grain sheds until they came to the prison wall.

'I don't want to be here,' said Moss, '*spying* on Eel-Eye Jack.'

Salter faced her. 'You think *I* do? Well there ain't no other way. You won't listen to me, so here we are. If I'm right, yer friend is payin Newgate a visit. And he ain't doin it out of charity.'

They'd lost sight of Eel-Eye Jack, but as they rounded the corner of the prison, there he was. Standing at the gatehouse, talking to the guard. Then he disappeared inside.

Moss let Salter pull her backwards into the crowd. She was still livid with him for spying on Eel-Eye Jack. But now she had to admit she was curious.

From behind the walls of the prison Moss could

hear noises – wailing and crying and the rattling of chains.

'I hate this place,' muttered Salter. 'It's misery an' fear an' neverendin dark. Tower of London ain't got nothin on Newgate. Next to Newgate, the Tower's a party.'

'Who do they lock up in there?'

'Thieves, murderers, debtors, monks. All sorts.'

'How come you know so much about it?'

Salter shrugged. 'If you've lived in this city long enough, you know about Newgate. You know that it's as close to hell on earth as you'll ever get. That the turnkeys starves them prisoners unless they pays up. That there ain't no windows, no light or air. That the floor is so thick with dead lice, you can hear the carcasses crunch like yer walkin on shells.'

The wailing and howling did not stop. The longer they stood there, the more Moss's head filled with the painful cries that leached from the cells beyond those stone walls.

'Let's go, Salter,' said Moss.

'No,' he said. 'We wait. See what happens when Eel-Eye comes out.'

'Why? What do you think he's doing in there?'

Salter drew breath, as though he couldn't quite bring himself to say what was on his mind. But he didn't have to, because at that moment, the massive doors of the gatehouse opened. Out came a man dressed in a long coat belted with a chain of heavy keys. He was followed by a shuffling prisoner, his back bent, his hands shackled in irons. Behind them both walked Eel-Eye Jack.

After a few short words, the jailer pushed the prisoner towards Eel-Eye Jack, who led him out of the gatehouse and away around the corner.

'There,' said Salter, a look of grim satisfaction on his face.

'What?' Moss was struggling to make sense of what she'd just seen.

'Eel-Eye Jack is buyin prisoners from Newgate and sellin them on to the Pit.

'What makes you think that?'

'The Whipmaster,' said Salter. 'When I saw him in the Pit last night, I thought to meself, I see him before.'

'Where?'

'In The Crow. He was there that first night an' again after we went to the Beast House.'

Moss scraped through the memory of those first few days at The Crow and Stump. There had been a man, though she'd not seen his face. The one who'd made the room quiet when he entered. The one who'd dropped the mutton bone. *The Whipmaster?* It could have been . . .

'But that doesn't mean he's doing what you say, Salter? All you've seen is Eel-Eye Jack leave Newgate with a man –'

'*Prisoner*,' corrected Salter.

'All right, even if he was a prisoner, you don't know that Eel-Eye Jack was taking him to the Pit. You didn't actually see him there last night, remember?'

Salter grabbed her by the shoulders. His grip was so tense that for a moment Moss thought he was going to shake her. His eyes burnt fierce brown and he held her so his face was just inches from her own.

'No,' he said, 'you have to listen to me . . .' His words were trembling and Moss realised that it wasn't anger, it was something else.

'Please,' he said, 'you have to –'

'Why are you so intent on dragging Eel-Eye Jack down? What has he ever done to you?'

'I don't care about *him*.' Salter loosened the grip on her shoulders. He still held her, but gently now, as though she'd turned into something that might break.

'What I mean is . . . I ain't doin this because of *him*.'

'Then why *are* you doing it, Salter? Do you even stop to look beyond yourself? You only see bad in Eel-Eye Jack. You think he's a thief or a scammer or I don't know what. You judge him, but you don't know anything about him. Well, I do. He plays music so beautiful it can stop your heart. He sees mountains in the clouds and sea in the rooftops. He understands people. He understands *me*.'

'Don't . . .' Salter's fierce eyes welled with tears. 'Don't say nothin more.' His arms dropped. 'I . . . I ain't . . .' His broken voice stumbled, unable to find the words. And Moss heard a wretched noise from deep in his chest and she gazed at him, too stunned to speak, because she had never seen Salter cry.

Then he turned and walked away from her, into the crowd.

She watched him go, trying to swallow the tightness that clamped her throat. Salter was her friend. Her first and only friend. For the year and a half that she'd known him, they'd been together almost every day. They'd fought and argued, they'd made each other hoot with laughter and a long time ago they'd saved each other's lives. He was so much a part of her, she could hardly remember what life was like before.

Why had all this changed?

Behind her the wailing, howling chorus from the dungeons rose to the skies.

Why had she said all those things? To make him understand? To hurt him? She could taste the bitter words in her mouth and she wished she could take them back. But she could not.

It took Moss longer than she'd imagined to find her way to the river. She'd thought she could catch Salter, but in the few moments she'd stood in the shadow of Newgate, he had vanished into the crowd.

On the shore now, she felt the familiar tread of shingle and mud beneath her boots and she hurried as quickly as she could in the direction of Belinsgate Wharf. She hoped that was where he was headed, but it was just a guess.

The fish market was in full flow. Up and down the gangways that served the jostling boats, sailors and fishermen heaved crates and rolled barrels, tipping fish and cockles onto the shore.

'Herring boats are comin!' came a cry from the wharf. 'Make way for the Hollanders!'

A ship was nudging its way in through the bobbing boats that clustered the wharf. An orange-capped sailor barked an order, gangplanks clattered and what seemed like a whole navy of sailors swarmed onto the quay. By the way they whooped and slapped each other, Moss guessed they had come in with a good catch.

Then she saw him. Salter. Weaving through the fisherman who packed the wharf and making his way towards the herring boat. He spoke to the sailor in the orange cap and in no time at all he was amid the crew, rolling barrels down the gangplanks. She watched, fascinated as he sprang from gangway to shore – steering the barrels and talking with the sailors as he went. She saw how easily he fitted with their boisterous banter. When the herring barrels were stacked, the orange-capped sailor beckoned him aboard the ship and Moss watched him climb the rigging to one of the beamed spars that crossed the main mast. His feet were nimble, finding their footholds as deftly as if he was running up stairs.

There he joined two men who stood on the spar, working to repair the broken rig.

Slowly it dawned on Moss that *this* was what Salter had been up to since they'd returned to London. All those mornings he'd left the tavern before breakfast, all those days when he'd been gone for hours on end. He'd been here at Belinsgate, working for the fishermen. So *this* was how he'd come by the money for the bread and cheese and the groat he'd offered for the Pit. He hadn't stolen it. He hadn't cheated people for it. He had earned it.

She'd believed the worst of Salter and had been completely wrong. She felt her face flush with the memory of her silent accusations. She'd kept them to herself, but deep down, she knew Salter must have guessed what she was thinking. And her silence must have hurt him all the more.

Now she wanted to cry out to him. But the shame of all she'd thought and said and done overwhelmed her. Her true friend. A friendship that she had broken. She had driven him away. She watched as he raised his head momentarily to gaze out over the river at a galley that was catching the turn of the tide, heading downriver for the open sea. What would he do now? Stay in London and work for the fishermen?

She heard the shouts of the Hollanders on the quayside as they loaded the empty barrels on to their ship and watched the deck fill with orange-capped sailors once more. They were getting ready to cast off. Salter seemed lost in his task, his head bent close to the wood of the mast. And suddenly, the scene before her made perfect sense.

Salter was leaving with the Hollanders. Joining them to chase shoals of herrings across the oceans for months on end. And after all she had done, perhaps he was better off without her? At least he would be safe, out on the open sea and away from the horrors of the dying river.

Moss turned her back to the quay, her eyes stinging with salt tears as she retraced her steps along the shingle. Her path led away from Salter, to the Isle of Dogs. To the Whipmaster.

A plan had begun to settle in her head. A way to do as the Riverwitch asked. What did she have to lose? She'd driven away her only friend. And although the thought of Salter gone from her life crushed her heart, she would not call after him now.

CHAPTER TWENTY
Bladder Street

No one saw her come and no one saw her go. The chattering crowd of The Crow and Stump ignored the girl in the green dress who moved like a ghost through the tavern.

Moss stood in the alley, a rust-red bundle tucked under her arm. She found a dark corner and changed out of her dress for Jenny Wren's boy clothes. She slipped the silver bird into the tunic pocket. As she folded the dress carefully she felt a sudden pang of longing for Pa. It couldn't be helped. She had a plan, and the soft woollen dress that Pa had given her would have to play its part.

It was well past noon by the time she reached Bladder Street and most of the sellers were packing up for the day. Trying to feel bold, she approached a man who was unpegging the last of his dried bladders from the line.

'Please. How much for one?'

The seller eyed her and sniffed. 'Twopence. Best bladders.'

Moss took a deep breath. She wasn't used to haggling and wished Salter was here. He'd be so much better at this than her. She screwed up her face in concentration, trying to think what he might have said.

'That's too much. I'll give you a farthing.' She felt her empty pocket, hoping it didn't look too empty.

'Are you deaf?' said the bladder seller. 'I said twopence. Now if you ain't got the money, then stop wastin me time and be on yer way.'

'Well,' said Moss, 'twopence seems like a lot for a bladder. Have you got all sizes?'

'Got big ones, small ones, thick ones, thin ones. If you got the money, you can take yer pick,' said the man. He delved into his sack and pulled out a small flat skin, more delicate than the rest. 'Lamb's bladder. Nice little wineskin fer a lady.' He eyed Moss's strange clothes. 'Or a young man. Well, d'you want it or not?'

Moss studied the bladder. 'I can see you have fine stock here. Do you prepare them all yourself?'

'Yes I do,' said the bladder seller. There's an art and a craft to choosin the right bladders. Got to know which ones make the best wineskins and which are good for water, got to hang em long enough to dry proper, but you don't want em goin hard as rock. And I works em supple with me own oil.'

'Really?'

The man nodded vigorously. 'You don't get that over in Eastcheap.'

'No,' said Moss. 'I expect there's a lot more to your craft than most people think.'

'That there is.' The bladder seller rubbed his hands, warming to Moss's interest. 'I learned from me father and he from his father before him. Third generation bladder seller, that's what I am,' he said proudly.

'That's impressive. My father's a weaver.' Moss patted the bundle under her arm. 'Wove this dress for a young lady in Thames Street and I was taking it to her, only when I got there she decided she didn't want green after all.'

The bladder seller looked at her blankly, unsure why they were suddenly talking about dresses.

'She was supposed to give me sixpence,' went on Moss, 'but I daresay we'll still be able to sell it for a groat. It's fine wool. Look.' She held out the folded dress. 'Maybe more.'

The bladder seller looked at the dress. Moss could see a slow calculation forming in his head.

'Tell you what,' he said. 'I can shift the dress for

you. I'll give you half a groat, right here right now. Then you won't be goin back to yer dad empty-handed.'

Moss shook her head. 'I don't know,' she said, 'I was supposed to get sixpence.'

'An' you got nothin,' said the man. 'Half a groat. Take it or leave it.'

'Maybe if you throw in one of those little bladders too?

'Half a groat and a bladder. Done.'

She almost couldn't bear to part with it. She remembered how happy it had made Pa when he'd given it to her. How tight she'd hugged him, knowing it was so much more than a dress. It was love and tenderness. The memory filled Moss with an ache for Pa and for the life she'd left behind.

The seller took the dress and gave Moss the money and the bladder.

Moss bit her lip. She had got what she'd come for. Her little story was a lie, but she was desperate, and she consoled herself with the knowledge that the bladder seller would not be out of pocket. Her dress really would fetch twice what he'd given her. And the half groat would buy her passage into the Beast House. There she'd hide and wait, just as before. And when she got to the Pit? The thought of what she planned to do made Moss want to cry out in fear.

CHAPTER TWENTY-ONE
Princess Redhead

Inside the Beast House, a handful of visitors crowded round the tiger's den. A keeper waved them away from the barred door, but Moss could hear their exclamations as they saw the mauled tiger with its injured paw.

She walked around them, heading for the white bear's den, then stopped. Sitting right up close, her slender fingers clutching the bars, was Elizabeth. She was gazing into the darkness of the den and from the way her lips moved, Moss could see that she was talking quietly to herself.

Curious, but not wanting to intrude, Moss squatted down next to her.

Elizabeth turned and at once her face lit up.

'I hoped I would see you,' she whispered. 'Every time I come to see the white bear, you are here too. Is there magic in you?'

Moss smiled. 'No magic,' she said, 'but I am glad to see you too.' She moved closer and peered into the den herself. The great white bear lay on his stomach, head low and hunched between his shoulders. The fur that a week ago had seemed so sleek and creamy white now hung from his body, ragged as a beggar's cloak. From deep in his chest came a noise that Moss hadn't heard in an animal before. A moaning. Soft and far away. A creature calling out in a place where it could not be heard.

'What's wrong with him? said Elizabeth. 'Is he crying?'

'I don't know if bears can cry,' said Moss. At the sound of Moss's voice, the bear opened one eye.

'He seems so tired,' said Elizabeth. 'I think they have not fed him at all today.' The little girl turned to face her and Moss saw that something had rubbed the brightness from Elizabeth's berry-brown eyes. Before she could ask, Elizabeth spoke.

'We came from Hampton Court,' she said. 'They let me see her. Just for a few minutes. She's really really sick . . .' She broke off.

'Who is sick?'

'The Queen.'

Then it dawned on Moss that Elizabeth was talking about her stepmother. Queen Jane, who'd given birth to Elizabeth's half brother less than two weeks ago and lay in bed with a fever that would not go away.

'Her skin was grey all over,' said Elizabeth. 'She could hardly move. Champers said all we can do is pray. So now I know.'

'Know what?'

'That she is dying.'

'Perhaps –'

'No perhaps,' said Elizabeth. 'I know that *all we can do is pray* means that she is going to die.'

Moss nodded. Not for the first time, she saw a child who spoke and felt way beyond her years.

'But I was bad,' said Elizabeth. 'I didn't say a single prayer. I ran from the room and when Champers caught me I told her I didn't want to pray because what was the point? She will die anyway. That's what happens to our mothers. Mine, Mary's, my baby brother's. They bring you into the world, then they leave you and they're gone forever.'

Moss felt for the silver bird in her tunic pocket. She brought it out, holding it carefully in the flat of her palm. It was warm, its sharp little beak glinting in the last rays of the sun.

'What's that?' said Elizabeth.

Moss held out her hand. 'It's a charm. It's yours.'

Elizabeth shook her head. 'I didn't lose a charm.'

'It was given to me by someone who loved you,' said Moss, 'and I believe she would want me to give it to you now.'

Moss took Elizabeth's hand and placed the little charm gently in it. 'You have to be careful,' she said, 'The beak is sharp and it'll cut your finger if you forget.'

Elizabeth turned the silver bird over in her hand. 'Did it bring you luck?'

Moss considered this. 'Yes, I think it did. My friend Salter thinks we make our own luck, and maybe we do, but it was a strange path that led me to the person who gave me that charm. And an even stranger one that has brought me to you.'

Should she tell her? There may not be another chance, thought Moss.

She watched Eizabeth tucking the silver bird into a purse that hung from the belt of her dress, her fingers fumbing the strings into an awkward bow. She was still so young. Moss tried to imagine herself in Elizabeth's place. Always wondering, what her mother was like, what she sounded like, what kind of things she said? Was she kind, was she happy? Did she used to sing? At least Moss had Pa's memories of her own mother. Even though the stories he told were the same over and over again, she never tired of hearing them. They comforted her.

'Elizabeth,' said Moss.

'Yes?'

'The silver bird . . . It was given to me by . . . Queen Anne. By your mother.'

Elizabeth stopped fumbling with her purse strings and stared at Moss.

'My mother?' At that moment, she looked more lost than Moss had ever seen her. A tiny, lost child.

'I met her. It was an accident; I was somewhere I shouldn't have been.'

'You met my mother?'

'It was in the King's Garden at Hampton Court.'

Elizabeth's face brightened. 'The one with the animals? With the golden lion and the falcon and the bull with its bulging eyes? I've sneaked in there so many times!'

'I was hiding in the garden,' said Moss, 'and your mother found me. She could have handed me over to the guards, but she didn't. She wasn't angry. She seemed . . .' Moss hesitated. 'She seemed curious.'

'Did you talk to her?' asked Elizabeth.

Moss nodded.

'Please tell me,' said Elizabeth, 'what did she say?' Her face was wide open, desperate for any scrap, anything at all about the person she had never really known.

'She told me she liked to hunt and play cards and that she could shoot a bow as well as any man. She told me she could make your father laugh. That he liked fun and mischief and that he'd never met anyone quite like her.'

'She made my father laugh?'

'She said she was . . . *different* to the ladies at court. That she spoke her mind and did things her own way.'

'Did she talk about me?'

'Yes,' said Moss, 'she called you her beautiful Elizabeth, her little Princess Redhead.'

'Princess Redhead . . .' The little girl stopped.

Elizabeth would have been nearly three when her mother died, thought Moss. 'Do you remember her at all?' she asked gently.

Elizabeth shook her head. A fat tear welled in the corner of her eye. Moss knew the hopelessness of that feeling. For the face she would never see and the hand she would never hold.'

Moss took Elizabeth's hand.

'Princess Redhead,' said the girl again, as if somewhere in her own words she might find the echo of her mother's voice.

'The Queen told me she loved you more than her own life.'

Elizabeth looked at Moss in wonder. 'She said that?'

Moss nodded and for a few moments the two girls were silent, side by side together on the cobbles.

'Then why did she leave me?'

'It . . . it all happened so quickly,' said Moss. 'I don't know. I don't know why they did what they did. Did anyone . . . tell you how?'

277

Elizabeth nodded and the tears ran down her cheeks.

'But listen,' said Moss, 'she loved you so much. She would have said goodbye if she could.' She wiped the tears from Elizabeth's cheek with the sleeve of her shirt. 'Of all the things she said to me that day, there is one that I will remember as long as I live. '

Elizabeth heaved a great sigh and scrunched her fists into her eyes. 'What thing?'

'That we must hold on to love. Wherever we can find it. I think it is the truest thing I have ever heard.'

'I don't know where to find it.'

'Perhaps you don't need to look too far. Maybe there is someone who is kind to you and cares for you and loves you as your mother would have done?'

For a moment Elizabeth looked blank.

'Elizabeth!' The call of the governess rang across the yard.

'*Champers!*' Elizabeth stared at Moss. But before she could really reply, the governess had hurried over to where the girls sat.

'Oh! Lady Elizabeth! That took forever! What a performance! The keeper insisted on sending a boy in to clean the garderobe before I could use it. And I have to say, even then it was an experience I would rather not repeat.' She sighed, 'Have you seen enough of your white bear, my little one?' She knelt down and opened her arms, drawing Elizabeth into her embrace. Then she seemed to notice Moss, and though she frowned slightly at the oddness of her clothes, the governess's expression was still kind. 'Did you make a friend?'

Elizabeth nodded. 'Champers, this is Moss.'

Champers smiled. 'Then I am pleased to meet you, Moss. We came here for some distraction on this very sad day. And I think perhaps you have given my Elizabeth some cheer.' She stood up. 'And now we will go. We have a long ride back.'

She stood up and Moss watched them walk together across the cobbled yard.

At the gate, Elizabeth pulled from the arm of her governess to wave. A tentative smile crept from under her battlefield curls and Moss found herself smiling too at the little girl who carried away the silver bird and a precious memory of her mother.

Moss looked around. She was alone. The last of the visitors had left just before Elizabeth and the keeper had scuffled out after the governess, hoping for a coin perhaps.

She peered through the barred door of the den and the great white bear lifted his head and sniffed, black nostrils flaring in the damp October air. A low throttling sound rumbled from his throat. Moss swallowed. The bear was looking straight at her, eyes dark and puzzled.

'Bear,' whispered Moss. 'Do you remember me?' She kept her voice as soft and comforting as she could. 'I am Moss and I came here before and I dressed your wound.'

The bear's ears flick-flacked left and right.

'I'm sorry that you are here. This prison is no place for a creature like you. Or for any of the others.'

The bear grunted. He looked drowsy, thought

Moss. There was a vinegary smell wafting from the den. To one side of the bear there was a large bucket, empty but for a puddle of dark red liquid at the bottom. *Wine*, thought Moss. She'd guessed right. Tonight they would take the great white bear to the Pit.

But just as she was about to climb through the feeding hatch, there was a shout from across the yard.

'Clear the yard, it's closin time now!'

She was too late.

Why hadn't she jumped into the den when she had the chance?

Cursing herself all the way out of the Beast House, she watched the keeper lock the gates, praying for some last minute miracle to let her nip back in.

CHAPTER TWENTY-TWO
An End to All This

Moss trudged down the path to the river. She'd blown it. With no time to walk to the Pit, how would she get to the Isle of Dogs now? Her plan was in pieces before it had even really begun.

On Tower Wharf there were a few people finishing their tasks for the day, mending, stacking and oiling. There were moored boats clanking against each other on the outgoing tide. Why hadn't she driven a harder bargain with the bladder seller?

A few more coins and she would have had enough to pay a waterman to row her down river.

'Hey!'

A voice along the wharf made her turn.

'Hey! Waterman! Here!'

It was a grey moonlit night, but the sheen of sand-blond hair was unmistakable.

Eel-Eye Jack! What was he doing here? Behind him shuffled a man, head bent. His hands were shackled. *The prisoner from Newgate?* She couldn't be sure.

Eel-Eye Jack was waving at a waterman who pulled on his oars to steer his boat in to the wharf. Was he taking the man somewhere? Eel-Eye Jack was talking to the waterman now. But, too far from the wharf to hear, Moss could not make out what they were saying.

As she watched, it occurred to her that there might be a way to find out. A trick. To know whether Eel-Eye Jack really had ever been to the Pit.

Quickly she braided her tangle-hair into two

long plaits, knotting a curl around each end to keep them in place. Delving into the pocket of the tunic, she brought out Jenny's Wren's scarf. It wasn't the startling pattern of scarlet flecked with gold daggers that Jenny had worn in the ring, but a vibrant red nonetheless. Moss pressed the scarf to her forehead and tied it at the back. Now, in all but the features of her face, she was Jenny Wren. In the shadows of the wharf, Eel-Eye Jack might not know the difference.

She walked towards him. 'Hey!'

Eel-Eye Jack turned and staggered back, as if he'd seen a ghost.

'Jenny?'

He knew Jenny Wren! He knew about the Pit. Had Salter been right all along?

She was just a few yards from Eel-Eye Jack now and the shock on his face had begun to drain away.

'But . . .' He shook his head in puzzlement. 'Moss? Is that you? I thought –'

'I know what you thought,' said Moss.

Before he could reply, the waterman yelled, 'Listen mate! Do you want this boat or not? Make yer mind up an' if you do, then it's cash up front. I don't go all the way to The Dogs on a promise.'

'Hold there, waterman.' Eel-Eye Jack pulled a pouch from his breeches and handed over two coins. He nodded to the prisoner. 'Get in,' he said. The prisoner did not protest. As if his feet were tied with rocks, he shambled to the boat and climbed in without a word.

Eel-Eye Jack and Moss stood facing each other on the wharf.

'I know what you are doing,' said Moss.

'Do you? Then you should have listened to your friend. I am not to be trusted.'

'This isn't about trust. It's about right and wrong. You can't take this man to fight in the Pit.'

'Why not? He will have his chance. The ones that live go free.'

'And the others? You have sent them to their deaths.'

'What do you know of death, Moss-from-the-village?'

'I know enough.'

'Then do you know what is worse than death?' He nodded at the prisoner in the boat. 'Look at him. He is a husk. His spirit has already left his broken body. Newgate took it from him, sucked out his soul until all he could do was wait for death's release. The torture of the body some can endure. But the torture of the mind is too much for any man.'

'I don't care. What you do is wrong, Jackin.'

'No, Moss, what I do is *necessary*.'

'How can it be necessary?'

He looked away. 'I will tell you,' he said, 'because I think you will understand.' His body rose and fell with a sigh from deep within. 'There is a man. And he will kill her if I do not . . .' In his eyes Moss could see something that looked almost like panic.

'If you do not what? Who will kill who?'

From the boat came an impatient yell. 'I ain't got

all night to wait fer you to finish chit-chatterin! If we're goin, let's go!'

'No time,' said Eel-Eye Jack.

'Wait!'

But he turned to climb into the boat.

'Jackin!' Moss moved to block his way. He stopped.

'Let me pass. I will not fight with you, Moss.'

'Don't do this.'

'I asked you once,' he said, 'what you see when you look at me?' He moved close to her now. So close she could feel the warmth of his breath on her cheek. '*This* is what I am. You see it now. All that I have done. All that I do –'

'No,' said Moss. 'I don't believe that. You dream of another life. You told me so on the rooftop. I hear it in your music.'

Eel-Eye Jack said nothing.

'It is not too late, Jackin,' she said. 'Leave this behind. Leave it in the past. My Pa once said to me, we must let the bad memories slip away, and make new, better memories to take the place of the old.'

Eel-Eye closed his eyes. She could not read him. She did not know what he was thinking. When he opened them again, he looked briefly up at the ink-black sky. At the moon, just visible through passing clouds. Then he pushed past her to the steps of the wharf and climbed into the boat.

'Thank the old Pope's footsores for that,' said the waterman, rolling his eyes. He took up his oars. But as the little vessel began to nudge its way to the edge of the wharf, a thought flashed into Moss's head.

The boat!

Three strides back, then she ran with all the strength and speed she could muster to the very edge of the wharf and launched herself into the air.

'Oi!' the waterman's goggle-eyes followed the arc of Moss's body, hurtling through the air towards him.

CRASH! With a cry and the clatter of tumbling bodies, Moss landed splat between Eel-Eye Jack and the open-mouthed waterman. The boat rocked wildly and hands flew to grab at the sides. Then the waterman, still gripping the oars, steadied the boat. At one end, the prisoner was hugging himself in a ball. Moss lay panting, while in front of her, Eel-Eye Jack picked himself up. His lip was bleeding. Moss scrabbled to her knees. 'I'm sorry,' she said, 'I –'

'It's just a split lip.' Eel-Eye Jack was looking directly at her. 'Why?'

'There is somewhere I need to be tonight.'

Eel-Eye Jack cocked his head to one side. 'We row to the Isle of Dogs. I will not alter our course. But once we are there, the waterman may take you where you need to go.'

'The Isle of Dogs is far enough for me,' said Moss.

The wind was behind them. The tide was carrying them. Moss reached into the pocket of her breeches. She felt the little bladder and its strange contents nestled between her fingers. On this object her fate now depended. She tried not to think about what could happen. Her only consolation was that Salter was safe. Probably halfway to Holland on a herringboat. She clung to this thought and it quelled the panic that rose within.

The closer they rowed to the Isle of Dogs, the more powerful the stench. The water was thick with the stinking mud and the waterman moaned and cursed with every stroke.

'Never seen the river this bad,' he muttered. 'Devil take that isle! A graveyard fer the rottin souls of men an' beasts that fell in the battles of old.'

Moss's ears pricked. 'What battles?' she said.

'Battles of long ago,' said the waterman. 'Too long ago for memory. Great battles, fought in the mud. The bodies of men and beasts, hacked and lifeless, sinking into the mire.'

Moss thought back to the Whipmaster's chilling prayer on the marsh. *One for bones of men asleep, One for blood in battle shed . . .* So this creature of the mud, this ancient evil, as the Riverwitch had called it, had it been kept alive by blood and bones of centuries past? And now the Whipmaster was feeding the Slider, it grew more and more powerful, turning the living river to mud, thick as guts.

'We are here,' said Eel-Eye Jack abruptly. 'Put into shore, waterman.'

The waterman steered the boat through the shallows and punted the last few feet through the mud with one oar.

'Wait with this passenger,' said Eel-Eye Jack, gesturing to the prisoner who was still curled at one end of the boat. 'Some men will come shortly to collect him.'

The waterman grumbled, but held his vessel steady while Eel-Eye Jack jumped out and hurried up the ramp onto the bridge. Moss sprang after him. Across the marsh she could see the torches of the Pit, flames clawing at the night sky. Moss forced herself forward and with every step, her heart pounded louder. She thought of the great white bear, roped and chained, waking slowly in some cramped cell to the sight of men poised with red-hot irons to prod him to his feet.

By the time she caught up with Eel-Eye Jack, they had crossed the bridge and the roar of the crowd swept through her like a raging storm.

'Why are you following me?' asked Eel-Eye Jack.

But Moss ignored his question. 'When we get to the gates, which way to Jenny Wren?'

Eel-Eye Jack stopped.

'What do you want with Jenny Wren?' His face had the same panicked look that she had seen on the wharf. 'She cannot be reached. She is a prisoner in the Pit.'

'I know, I –'

'Do you think I haven't tried to free her?'

Free her? A thought clicked in Moss's head. A memory of something Eel-Eye Jack had told her. *I knew a bold girl once . . .* The girl who'd run away. Eel-Eye Jack's friend. *Jenny Wren?*

'Why do you think I do this?' he said. 'Bring these men here? For money?' For a moment Moss thought Eel-Eye Jack was going to spit in the mud.

'*Not* for money. I do this because if I don't, he will kill her.'

'He?' said Moss in a small voice.

'The one they call the Whipmaster. I offered him money to release her. But then he saw my weakness. And he has exploited it ever since. So long as I bring him the prisoners from Newgate, Jenny lives.'

'But she could be killed at any time in the ring by the animals,' said Moss.

'What choice do I have? At least in the ring, she has a chance.' He set his fierce blue eyes on Moss. 'But one day I will find a way. I will free her.'

'One day?' said Moss. 'How about *today*?'

Jackin began walking towards the Pit again. 'Impossible. She is guarded until it is time for her fight.'

'No,' said Moss. 'Not always. When the beasts arrive from the Tower, there's time.'

'The keepers will stop me before I get within ten paces of where she is kept.'

'But they won't stop *me*. I *am* Jenny Wren! Well,

293

maybe in the shadows. And perhaps if I can find her, I can get her out.'

Eel-Eye Jack looked as if he would have laughed, only his face was creased with too much pain.

'Wait on the shore,' said Moss. 'Keep the boat there if you can. I will find a way to get her out. I'll tell her you are there.'

As they approached the guards on the gate, Eel-Eye Jack called to them.

'The man for tonight is in the boat. Tell Severs.'

One of the guards called through the gate and two men hurried out and across the bridge to collect the prisoner.

Once more Eel-Eye Jack put his hand on Moss's arm.

'What do you hope to achieve, Moss-from-the-village?

'An end,' said Moss. 'An end to all this.'

'How can one girl end all this?' he said. 'Go back now. You cannot stop it. He is too strong. His power comes from another place. If you go on, it

294

will not be his end, it will be yours.'

Moss shook off his hand. 'I have to try,' she said.

She bent her head as she approached the guards on the gate.

'Stop right there!' said one. 'What you doin out on the marsh? You ain't allowed out of the Pit. Whipmaster's orders.'

'Let me pass,' growled Moss in her best attempt at Jenny Wren's voice, 'Fight will be startin soon an' you don't want to have to answer to *him* if I ain't there, do you?'

'She's got a point, Joe,' said the other guard

They let her through. No one wanted to get on the wrong side of Severs.

Alone in the earthen passageway, Moss walked swiftly towards the large wooden door at the end. Last time she was here, she'd been on the other side of this door. Behind it this time, she figured, would be a sleeping bear and a girl getting ready for a fight.

She pushed at the door, then leaned into it using the weight of her body. It was heavy, but it swung open and Moss found herself standing in the same cell as before. Sitting in the flickering torchlight on a low bench was Jenny Wren. At once she sprang up, her eyes wide in shock at the sight of her double standing before her. Before Moss could even begin to explain, the girl's knife was at her throat.

'Steal my clothes, would you? Dress like me an' come back fer more?'

'Wait! Let me speak!'

Jenny Wren took the knife from Moss's throat and poked it under the scarlet scarf, flicking it deftly from Moss's head and catching it in her hand.

'Speak now then,' she said. 'They'll be comin for me soon. And unless it's a fight in the Pit you wants, you'd better not be here when they do.'

CHAPTER TWENTY-THREE
Bear Fight

'JE-NNY WREN! JE-NNY WREN! JE-NNY WREN!'

All around the arena the savage cries were building to a roar.

'JE-NNY WREN!'

Anyone who looked closely at the girl in the red-leather tunic would have seen that something was not quite right.

She wore her mask as usual, her silk scarf knotted at the back, her hair braided in two plaits. But something was different. Perhaps it was the way she ran and leapt. Perhaps it was the colour of her hair. The shape of her face.

No one noticed.

Moss slipped her hand under the skin-tight mask to wipe the sweat that was now running freely down her forehead. In her tunic pocket was the little bladder. In her boot was a knife.

At first, Jenny Wren had spluttered disbelief at Moss's request to give up her mask, her knife and her place in the Pit. But when Moss had talked of Eel-Eye Jack waiting for her on the shore and the chance for them all to be free of Severs, she had agreed.

Jenny had taken off her red tunic. She'd stood before Moss in her breeches and white shirt, then handed over her knife.

'Go on then,' she'd said, and watched with amusement while Moss had cut off Jenny's long plaits, roughing her hair to a boyish mop.

'There. No one will recognise you now.'

Jenny's face had become suddenly grave.

'You know what I fights tonight?'

Moss nodded.

'A great white bear ain't no wolf.'

'I know.'

Jenny had handed Moss her leather mask. Then she'd stepped forward, tied the scarlet and gold scarf around Moss's head and stood back to look.

'There. It's like lookin at meself.'

'Will anyone know the difference?' said Moss.

'Nah,' said Jenny. 'Those brutes will all be beered up an' howlin an' they won't see nothin but their own bloodlust.'

'Thank you,' said Moss. 'I won't forget this.'

Jenny had shaken her head. 'You saved my life in the ring with that tiger. An' I can't say that I feel like I'm returnin the favour. You sure you want to go through with it?'

But before Moss could answer, they'd heard the shouts of men from the passage. Jenny dived under the bench. Moss lowered her face as the men came in.

'Hope yer ready fer this one, Little Wren.'

Moss had followed them down the flickering passage, the bellow of the crowd tearing at her ears, until there she was. Standing in the ring.

'BEAST! BEAST! BEAST!'

Moss stared up. All around her, a dizzying stack of faces howled, grotesque mouths opening and closing. She staggered back. From somewhere, deep in the bowels of the Pit, a mighty roar shook the earth walls.

On all sides of the arena, men poured through the gates, some carrying flaming torches, some grasping the long metal rods that burned red-hot at the ends. Two carried a brazier of smoking coals, stuck through with more rods, which they set at the side of the ring.

'BEAST! BEAST!'

Moss's throat was dry as ash.

From the corner of her eye she caught a flash of white. It was Jenny Wren, clambering to the lip of the terrace.

The tall gates flew open. Unfettered and unbound, the great white bear crashed into the arena. His mouth was open, saliva dripping from his black lips. In the roll of his eyes, Moss saw terror and confusion at the noise all around, at the flaming torches that swiped at his fur and the wall that rose up and up, a circling prison of mud.

Then the bear threw back his head and roared to the sky.

The crowd erupted.

'FIGHT! FIGHT!'

Moss ran for the wall as the bear lumbered towards her with surprising speed. Realising she would not make it in time, Moss turned to see the bear rear up on his hind legs. He towered above her, a trunk of matted fur, tall as a tree, his massive underbelly stretching his body to its full height. With a force that could have smashed a ship in two, he brought his mighty bulk down on his two front paws. In the split-second before they crashed down on top of her, Moss sprang to the side, rolling to her feet and clawing her way up the slope of the mud wall to the terrace.

There she hovered, panting, while all around the yells and cheers grew louder. The Whipmaster lay back on the skins of his mud throne. This is what they had come to see. And soon his creature, the Slider, would be fed again.

Moss felt the anger welling in her chest. She gulped the cold air, trying to steady her breath and her thoughts. *Stick to the plan*, she told herself. *It's all you've got.*

A shove from behind sent her tumbling back down into the arena. She lashed out, digging her hands into the earth walls to slow her fall. At the bottom she staggered to her feet, her head whirling, fuzzy shapes coming at her from all directions. And as the ring came into focus, she saw the hulking bear coming towards her once more.

'Bear!' Moss cried. 'Bear, it's me!' Her words were lost in the bellow of the crowd. But at the sound of her voice, the bear paused. He raised his head and sniffed the air.

Moss took a tentative step forward. She was about to reach out her hand for the bear to smell, when the lightning crack of a whip ricocheted around the ring. Severs was standing on the edge of the terrace, whip at his side. He lashed again. The sudden crack startled the bear and he lurched forward. All Moss saw was a blur of fur, the swipe of the bear's mighty paw. It thumped into her side, knocking the breath from her chest and the force of the blow sent her tumbling over and over to the edge of the ring. When she looked up, the great white bear was standing over her, eyes fathomless in the torchlight. And Moss knew that this was the end. In her tunic pocket, she touched the little bladder. Her fingers tugged at the string around its neck. Severs was so very far away. But this little skin pouch and its contents might bring him to her. In her boot was Jenny Wren's knife.

Moss picked herself up and stood before the bear. She tried to block the noise of the arena from her ears. Time slowed as she saw him lift and turn his head in one graceful movement, his mighty jaw yawning wide to a bite that Moss knew could snap her body like a stick. But Moss was quick. Ducking the jaws, she threw herself at the mat of fur that was the bear's neck, clinging to it, calling in his ear once more.

'Bear! It's me! The one who slept in your cage, who tended your bleeding ear.' She plucked the tiny bladder from her pocket. 'Bear, it's me, Moss!'

No one could hear her through the din of the crowd. They yelled for Jenny Wren, whistling and stamping their feet. They saw her, wrapped round the neck of the great bear, locked in what must surely be some crazed death embrace, for the creature was raging and hungry and the girl stood no chance.

They saw the fighting girl fall. They saw her hit the ground. She rolled over and they saw the mess of blood spreading beneath her tunic, staining the white of her shirt deep red. The men rushed forward, thrusting the flaming torches at the great white bear, herding him to one side of the ring.

'WHIPMASTER! WHIPMASTER!'

The gathering storm of voices raised Severs from his throne and he made his way down the steps to the ring.

Lying on the dirt floor, Moss was still, her hand against her chest. She felt the wetness, a spreading stain that soaked her tunic. She pressed her fingers to the sticky blood. In the space between her tunic and her shirt, she felt the little bladder, its contents spilled. Cow blood. Scooped from the buckets of the butchers alley, stored in the little bladder. She'd tied it tight with string so not a drop would escape until she was ready. It had worked better than she ever could have hoped.

'WHIPMASTER! WHIPMASTER!'

Through the dust and smoke, she saw the Whipmaster, striding towards her. She could feel the knife, wedged between her leg and the leather. She lay very still.

Severs stopped in front of her. He raised his

head, drinking in the noise, then he bent down, knee in the dirt behind her.

Slowly, imperceptibly, Moss's hand slid inside her boot. She felt the leather mask slip a little. It must have come loose when she'd fallen from the great white bear. She could feel Severs bending towards her. The handle of Jenny's knife was cold to her touch.

Inside her now, Moss felt icy fingers reaching down to her heart. Numbing her. Wrapping themselves around anything they could find that was warmth or kindness. And as she began to draw the knife, she knew that if she went through with this act, no matter how cruel this man was, no matter how much suffering he had caused, if she killed him, there was no going back. It would change her. The numbness would never leave. The ice-fingers would stay wrapped around her heart forever.

She could not do it.

The Whipmaster grabbed Moss by the red silk

scarf, jerking her head up. The sudden movement made her mask drop to the floor.

For a moment Severs was speechless at this unexpected face.

'What?' he hissed. 'Not the Little Wren?'

'LEAVE HER ALONE!'

From high above Moss, a voice came hurtling towards her. A figure, half running, half rolling down the slope of the wall.

'GET OFF HER! GET AWAY FROM HER!'

Salter?

She couldn't believe what she was seeing. Sprinting across the ring towards her was Salter. With a flying leap he launched himself at Severs, kicking and punching and bowling him backwards with the rush of his body.

'Salter!' Moss sprang to her feet and saw Jenny Wren jump from the lip of the terrace, graceful as a deer. The girl seized a flaming torch from a bracket and pelted down the slope, flames and smoke trailing in her wake.

'Argghh!' Severs threw Salter into the dirt and scrabbled back to pick up his whip.

From the other side of the ring, the bear growled, still penned by the men with torches.

CRASH!

The wicker gate flew open and a blur of sand blond hair streaked towards them. *Eel-Eye Jack?* It all happened so quickly. Eel-Eye Jack snatched two irons from the brazier and launched one into the air towards Salter. Salter raised both hands. The rod smacked into his palms and he pulled it deftly to his body.

Now they stood. The four. Moss, Salter, Jenny Wren and Eel-Eye Jack. Backs to each other, facing out towards the ring. Moss gripping the knife, Jenny her flaming torch, Salter and Eel-Eye Jack holding the rods in front of them like swords.

The Whipmaster was picking himself up from the mud, wiping the blood from a cut above his eye where Salter had punched him. Behind him, men with clubs advanced towards the four.

Severs raised his hand. His men stopped. 'Leave them. Let the bear do its work and the Slider will feast tonight.'

He turned and walked from the ring. Moments later he was back on the terrace, settling in for the fight. On one side of the ring the great white bear growled, shaking his muzzle at the men still holding him back. Above her head, Moss heard the whip crack. The men backed away from the bear carefully, holding their torches at arms length.

'Put down your weapons,' said Moss quietly to the others and she laid her knife on the ground.

'Are you crazy?' said Jenny Wren.

'Let him see you do it,' said Moss. 'He must not be afraid of us. If he is not afraid, he will not hurt us.'

'You know the mind of a bear?' said Eel-Eye Jack.

'Just do as she says,' said Salter, 'unless you got a better plan?' He tossed his iron rod into the mud. 'I've said it before, she's crazier than a full-moon stoat. But I'll tell you somethin else – I wouldn't change that, not fer all the coins in Henry's coffers.'

'Salter.' She turned towards him. Her mud-streaked face caught the warmth of his brown eyes. He hadn't left her. In spite of everything she'd said. He'd come back.

Next to them, Eel-Eye Jack dropped his iron rod and Jenny Wren pushed her flaming torch into the mud. The flames went out, leaving a thin mist of grey smoke. They stood now, the four, in a huddle, the great wooden gates behind them. On the other side of the ring, the bear arched his neck and whined.

'Get behind me,' said Moss. 'Stay there and be ready to run.'

'Run where?' said Jenny Wren.

'Out of here. Just be ready,' said Moss. 'Bear!'

The white bear looked up and his eyes were blank. He tossed his head, confused. The men with the biting fire sticks had gone. But here was the small one whose scent he knew.

Moss took a few steps towards him. Gently she lifted her hand, held out her palm. The bear sniffed.

'This way, bear,' said Moss. 'Come on!'

Behind her, Eel-Eye Jack and Jenny Wren moved to run from the path of the advancing bear, but Salter grabbed their wrists.

'Not yet! Wait for her signal. She knows what she's doin.'

'This way!' called Moss and the bear lumbered forward again. The four of them were backed against the high wooden gates, Moss in front. The great white bear lifted himself high on two legs and his roar split the night air.

'Sweet Mary's teeth,' breathed Salter. And just as the bear was about to bring the weight of his body down, Moss screamed.

'RUN! NOW!'

They ran. Moss and Salter darting to the right, Eel-Eye Jack and Jenny Wren to the left, as the mighty bulk of the great white bear smashed down on the wooden gates, shattering them into a thousand splinters and opening a gaping hole to the world outside.

'GO!' cried Moss. She flung herself at the bear, grabbing at tufts of thick fur, heaving herself right up on to the bear's back. She wrapped her arms as tight as she could, clinging with all her strength as the beast lurched forward through the splintered gates.

'Go!' she cried again and she heard the bear snort, heard his deep throttling breaths as he leapt through the smashed gates. Out into the darkness beyond the Pit.

CHAPTER TWENTY-FOUR
The Slider Rises

Behind Moss, the yells of men filled the air. The crack of a whip. She didn't look back. She didn't have to. She could hear them spilling from the Pit. She knew they came with torches and irons, driven by the Whipmaster.

'RUN, BEAR!' she cried into the bear's ear.

This creature could not possibly understand. But his powerful legs ploughed into the mud. In the distance the river slapped against the shore – waves that pitched and tossed, even though there was not a breath of wind.

'See?' cried Moss, 'The river!'

The bear snorted. Her fingers burrowed into the thick fur. She must not fall. They must reach the river. And Moss knew that somewhere the Riverwitch was out there, waiting. But she also knew that no matter how angry were the waves that beat the shore, while the Whipmaster lived, the Witch had no power over the Slider.

The bear was slowing, his huge paws heavy and the weight of his body sinking with every stride. Though his strength was great, the mud was dragging him down. The shouts of men were closing in on them. Moss looked up and saw them running along the high bridge from the Pit.

'Keep going!' she cried. They couldn't have been more than twenty yards from the shore now. But the bear was tiring rapidly, groaning in the thick mud that stopped his passage to the river.

From the bridge came the cry of the Whipmaster. A cry that seemed to come from some unearthly place. Not the cry of a man, but the cry of something that had shed its human voice. And she could not help but look.

The Whipmaster stood, on the edge of the bridge, his arms raised, his whip stretched taut between them. His eyes were closed, but his mouth was moving. All around him, the men with their torches fell silent. The Whipmaster's cry pierced the air.

One to open marshland deep
One for bones of men asleep
One for blood in battle shed
One for a beast without a head
One to turn them all to mud
One to lift the dark's bent hood
One for the chaos that will rise
For none can stop the Slider

All at once, Moss felt herself tip forward. The ground was shifting. The mud was changing. Rising and falling, the slow arc of something powerful coming up from deep inside the earth. The great white bear staggered, his legs floundering in the grip of the cloying mud.

'No!' cried Moss. 'Don't stop –' But before she could finish, the bear's weight was thrown to one side as the earth erupted in a rolling wave of mud. Moss screamed. Above them, the Whipmaster called out.

'COME, MY CREATURE! FROM THE DEPTHS SHALL YOU RISE!'

All around them, the earth groaned and sucked, ripping itself apart as though pulled by some massive force.

'COME TO ME!'

From deep in the gaping chasm came the Slider. A slow coil of muscle, unfurling before them, pulsing with suckers, black and glistening. Up and up it rose, thick as the trunk of a great oak, its body slick with mud. Against the night sky a blunt head reared. Where its eyes should have been were two hollow sockets stretched with skin. The unmade eyes of a newborn creature.

Moss could not move. Beneath her the bear was stuck fast. Her fingers gripped his neck tight. She wanted to bury her head in the mud-spattered fur, but could not tear her gaze from the Slider. Its head seemed to split in two, jaws opening as wide as a portcullis. Its teeth were stone, rooted in the flesh of its maw, trailing strands of muddy saliva as its mouth gaped wide. A creature from the otherworld, a creature of earth and mud and rock, made living flesh by the man who called its name from the bridge.

'SLIDER! COME TO ME!'

The creature turned, sensing its master. Slowly, the great coil of its body slithered towards the bridge It swayed upwards, feeling its way towards the Whipmaster's voice.

'See what I have for you!'

The men on the bridge shrank back at the approach of the Slider, but Severs stayed where he was. From a sack, he pulled a dead dog and dangled it by its legs over the rail of the bridge. It hung there for no more than a second before the creature's wide jaws snapped around it. Moss heard the crack of bones and the Slider pulled back.

A satisfied smile crawled across Severs' face and he drew himself up. The Slider had risen. A creature that slithered from the mud to do his bidding.

'Finish them,' hissed the Whipmaster.

A strange silence engulfed the marsh. A suffocating silence that smothered the sky and the stars and everything below.

Moss felt the bear shudder as the creature moved towards them. She saw the Slider's head swaying slowly from side to side. Under the blind sockets, a bulging mass pushed, stretching the skin drum-tight until they were almost translucent. The Slider was close to them now, turning this way and that, as if trying to sense their presence. Then, across the marsh, the silence was punctured by the sudden rip of flesh. The creature's eye sockets had split. Two bulging eyes burst through the skin. The yellow eyes of a serpent, swivelling in their sockets, bulbous, slashed from top to bottom by a black slit.

The Whipmaster craned over the bridge to see his creature, drinking in its power as it sloughed through the mud, encircling the girl and the bear. His creature had been denied its meal from the Pit, but now it would feed. It would grow stronger. Strong enough to choke the river and turn all to mud.

'WAIT!' Severs' voice cut through the night.

The Slider was still.

Severs turned to his men. 'Bring the Little Wren to me. And the other one!'

There was a scuffling on the bridge and Moss saw Salter dragged before the Whipmaster, Jenny Wren behind, each held fast by Severs' men.

'Get yer filthy paws off me, you cussin bag of rat-nubbers!' yelled Salter, struggling to wrench his arms free. But the men were strong. There were many of them. And though Jenny Wren managed to land a sharp kick to the stomach of one, neither she nor Salter could break their grip.

'Thought you could flee my nest, Little Wren?'

the Whipmaster hissed. 'What's the matter? Did fear catch up with you?'

Jenny Wren spat at Severs' feet. 'I ain't afraid of you, nor nothin. I'll fight you or any one of yer stupid men, any time you like.'

'The time for fighting is over, Little Wren.'

He turned to Salter. 'And you . . .'

The men thrust Salter forward, forcing him to his knees in front of Severs. 'You dare to attack the Whipmaster?'

Salter said nothing. Still trying to wrench himself free, he glowered at Severs.

'Your silence will not save you,' said the Whipmaster. 'Bring Jack!'

Through the flickering torches, Moss saw two men push Eel-Eye Jack before Severs.

'Eel-Eye Jack,' sneered Severs. 'A faithful dog, turned against its master. Tell me, dog, do you know this boy?'

'I know him. He's a river thief. A scammer. He makes a living from the misfortune of others,' said Eel-Eye Jack, 'just like me.'

'I ain't NOTHIN like you!' yelled Salter, his face raging at this sudden betrayal. 'You're a snake-tongued cheater who'd sell yer own brother!'

'I like cheats,' said Severs, 'and I like thieves too. They're smart enough to know what's coming. And always looking for a way out, eh, Jack?'

He gestured to his men. They let go of Salter and Eel-Eye Jack and formed a semicircle around the platform to block any chance of escape down the bridge. In front of them Severs stood, unfurling his whip. Meanwhile a wooden club was brought and placed in the hands of Eel-Eye Jack.

'Strike the river thief from the bridge. Into the jaws of my creature. Deliver him to the Slider and you shall go free.'

'No!' Moss's voice was a thin, pleading note, calling up to Eel-Eye Jack. But her cry was lost in the mud as she clung to the bear while the ground rumbled and shifted beneath them. The Slider was moving. Uncoiling itself, it slithered away from

Moss, across the marsh. The trunk of its neck stretched upwards towards the bridge, jaws gaped wide in a hiss that was hunger and lust for the flesh that its master promised.

On the platform, Salter was kicked forward by Severs and scrabbled to his feet, circling Eel-Eye Jack.

'I ain't goin without a fight!' he cried, 'Come on then, you stinkin piece of dogmeat!'

'NO!' yelled Moss. She gripped the fur of the great white bear and watched, helpless as Eel-Eye Jack raised the club and swung it back, ready to strike Salter.

'JACKIN, STOP!'

With a sudden twist of his body, Eel-Eye Jack hurled himself in the opposite direction, swiping low with the club. There was a crack and a yell of pain as the club struck the Whipmaster's knees, knocking him from his feet, just as Salter threw himself at Severs. The two of them rolled over and over to the very edge of the platform.

'SALTER!' screamed Moss as they went over the edge. At the same time, Eel-Eye Jack dived forward, grabbing a bridge-post with one hand and Salter's arm with the other.

She saw Severs fall from the bridge, then jerk to a stop in mid-air, thrashing backwards and forwards, his hands still clutching the whip. It had snagged on a cleft of wood.

Beneath the bridge, the jaws of the Slider yawned wide. Up it rose, the gulf of its mouth rooted with teeth ready to grind a body to powder.

'COME ON!' yelled Eel-Eye Jack, heaving to get Salter's body back up on to the bridge.

The Slider's eyes fixed themselves on Salter's dangling legs. Then it lunged, the powerful thrust of its trunk propelling it through the air, twisting its head, jaws closing, Salter's legs still thrashing.

SNAP!

There was a sickening crunch of bone.

Moss screamed.

Salter's legs disappeared up and on to the platform

of the bridge. He sprang to his feet and instantly Eel-Eye Jack pulled him back from the edge.

Under the platform, the ragged handle of the whip swung back and forth, torn by the force of the Slider's bite. And where the Whipmaster had swung from its handle was nothing but empty air.

The bile rose in Moss's stomach as the creature ground the contents of its mighty jaw to dust.

'MOSS!' yelled Salter from the bridge. 'GET BACK! GET OFF THE MUD!'

He was staring wildly in the direction of the river.

Out beyond the mud-flats, something was happening. As the grey clouds blew clear of the moon, the water was lit suddenly by a shaft of silver light. The river was moving. A green-black torrent was surging towards them. Pouring into the dips and swells of the marsh and gathering speed as it went.

'Get ready, bear,' whispered Moss. The bear raised his head and she felt his body stiffen.

Out on the river frost fingers of foam arched high, two curling walls of water, reaching forward across the marsh. The Riverwitch was coming.

Next to the bridge the Slider turned and its eyes fixed on the rush of the green-black river. It reared up, its hiss searing the night as the force of the water knocked it sideways, ripping it from the mud, watery fingers around its throat.

Moss dug her fingers into the bear's fur and closed her eyes.

Then the river hit them, tumbling her from the bear's back, over and over in the blackness, before dragging her to the surface. She flailed her arms, thrashed her legs, anything to keep her head above water. Through the spray of the gathering waves, she could see the bridge. And she could see that the force of the flood was pushing at the wooden posts that held it. All along its length, men were running back towards the Pit, torches still blazing, trying to get off. On the high platform, Salter, Jenny Wren and Eel-Eye Jack braced themselves, arms wrapped around a stout post that Moss knew would be their only hope of survival when the bridge collapsed.

Now the bridge was groaning. The wood was shifting. She heard Salter yelling to the others.

'HANG ON! HERE SHE GOES!'

Moss wanted to cry out, but no cry would come. She watched, helpless, as one after another the huge timbers of the bridge tumbled like the slow felling of trees. She saw the platform break apart, planks dropping into the water. She saw Salter falling, still clinging to the wooden post. Then he was lost to the raging swirl of the river.

Moss kicked her legs and lunged with her arms, struggling to find a way out of the waves that engulfed her now. But as she fought her way upwards, through the murk, came a shape. A muscular trunk, snaking towards her. Churning the water with its powerful body, dredging mud from the depths to quell and choke the river. Closer it came, a gaping darkness, a hunger for flesh and bone. Somewhere in the noise of the river she heard her own scream. And there in front of her was the Slider, ready to grind and crush and swallow.

But as the mighty jaw thrust forward to take its prey, Moss felt herself propelled upwards. Lifted by some unseen force towards the grey light. A rush of water tore at her body, an explosion of power bursting through the surface of the wave. Choking and flailing, she grabbed at anything she could and found that her fingers clutched fur.

The great white bear! His body pushing through the surging river, his paws ploughing the water, his back broad and strong, bearing her away from the creature.

In front of them now the waves were climbing like sheer cliffs. Inside them, rising with the tumbling water, was the Riverwitch, lifting her arms until the crests of the waves were high enough to block the stars. And Moss knew that the Witch summoned all the power of the raging river and that her fight with the Slider would be to the death.

Next to them, the head of the Slider erupted from the depths, a blur of flesh and teeth, riverweed trailing from its suckers. As it rose from the river, the waves came hurtling down, powerful fists of water that pounded the creature until its body began to break apart. From it fell rocks, earth and the bones of men and beasts. And in among the waves, Moss saw the Riverwitch, surging with the torrent, her arms no longer blackened, but strong as white stone. The Witch and the river were one, crushing the mighty trunk of the Slider, smothering its jaw and smashing it from side to side, before plunging the creature deep down. The last Moss saw of the Slider was its tail, flailing feebly before it, too, was dragged into the shadow-depths.

Moss buried her head in the bear's fur.

The Slider was gone.

Across the water, the waves calmed to a gentle swell.

Moss felt herself lifted from the bear's back, floating on a current that pulled her just beneath the surface. She had not time to draw breath, but instead of choking, a calmness shot through her veins and her body was still. Suspended in the inky depths she felt the ice-river running through her, *inside* her.

River Daughter . . .

There in front of Moss was the torn face of the Riverwitch, inches from her own.

You kept your bargain . . . you are free . . .

The Witch's voice whirled around her.

The river is in you . . .

Moss saw two arms reaching out towards the Witch. They were hers. The river was inside her, flowing through her veins, warmed by the blood that pumped from her heart. She touched the Witch's cheek. It was hardly there. Just a flutter of skin. But as her fingers felt the tattered fronds, she could see something was happening. Piece by piece, over bare bone and teeth, the fragments of a face that had once been were knitting themselves together.

Moss heard her own gasp echo in the water.

In front of her now was pale, smooth skin. The face of a young woman.

The Witch reached out and stroked Moss's face,

sadness and longing in her lantern eyes.

River Daughter . . .

Then she drifted backwards and the grey river swirled around her fading body until Moss could see the Riverwitch no more.

The bear was beside Moss now and, with great effort, she grasped its leg and managed to clamber on to its back. All around them bobbed the wreckage of the Pit and the bridge, with men clinging to whatever pieces they could find.

Moss scrambled to her knees, grasping a tuft of fur with one hand and scouring the river for any sign of Salter. She called his name, but all she heard was her voice over the water.

The great white bear turned and began to swim downriver. Away from the Isle of Dogs. Away from the Tower. *To the sea*, thought Moss. For beyond the sea lay the cold countries. The great white bear was swimming home. She laid her head on the bear's neck. Closing her eyes, she felt the powerful body heaving itself through the current, the pull of his homeland giving his limbs new life.

Then, faint, snatched by the wind came a voice. Moss's head jerked up. There it was again. Louder now. Unmistakable. Calling her name.

'Leatherboots!'

'Salter? SALTER! WHERE ARE YOU?'

Through the waves she saw him now. Lit by the grey moon, a speck in the swell. Clinging to the broken bridgepost and kicking towards her.

As if he understood, the bear slowed his stroke.

'Bear,' Moss whispered. She thought of Big Sal and Farmer Bailey. *A rare friendship*, Pa had called it. The great white bear had saved her life. She wondered whether Pa would ever believe it if she told him. 'Goodbye, bear,' she said. She laid her hand on the bear's head, stroking the soft, wet fur between his ears. From somewhere deep inside his body she felt a rumble, and though she could not be sure, she wondered if the bear was talking back. She nuzzled her face deep into the wet fur of the bear's neck, before slipping into the water.

Only when she began to swim did she realise how exhausted she was. She heard the splash of Salter kicking towards her and she could see his face full of fear and relief, eyes that didn't leave her for one second. When she reached him, still with one arm wound around the bridgepost, Salter scooped her up, pulling her tight so she could feel the warmth of his face against hers. Freezing though she was, Moss wrapped her arms round him and wished the world would stop so she could hold this moment as tight as she held Salter himself.

There they stayed until a cry broke through the night. Crouching on the wreckage of a shattered gate was Jenny Wren, eyes wide and hair plastered to her face.

At first, none of them spoke. It was Salter who broke the silence.

'Eel-Eye –'

Jenny Wren shook her head.

'Perhaps . . .' said Moss, but she couldn't finish her thought. All of them knew that many would have died in the river that night, struck by the falling timber, dragged down by the current, caught up in the struggle between the Riverwitch and the Slider.

She reached for Jenny's hand and held it tight. Then she felt Salter's hand on hers. All she could hope was that Eel-Eye Jack's end had been quick and without pain.

'Come on,' said Salter. 'We've got to get off the river. Find somewhere warm an' dry.'

As they paddled away from the Isle of Dogs, Moss turned to look back. The clouds had vanished. Far away and lit by the moon, as bright as snow, she spotted the great white bear. Moving slowly through the water. But there was something else too.

On the bear's back!

Not something. *Someone.* Clinging to the bear. And though the figure was just a dark smudge against white fur, Moss was almost sure. That riding on the back of that great white bear was a boy with a longing for the cold countries that he called home.

Eel-Eye Jack.

CHAPTER TWENTY-FIVE
Boat of Leaves

The first thing Moss saw when she opened her eyes was a gold-edged sun, peeping through the shutters of the tiny room at the top of the tavern.

It must have been close to midnight by the time they'd put to shore. Despite Moss's protests, Jenny Wren had said goodbye and set off alone. Salter had offered to pay for a warm room for them all, but Jenny had insisted on going her own way. She said she would wait at Broken Wharf for a ship that would take her to the lands across the northern seas. There she would begin a search for her friend Eel-Eye Jack.

The room was cosy. There was a fire and Moss knew Salter must have paid extra for it to be lit. They'd hung their clothes to dry and huddled together in their blankets with their backs to the flames until Moss sank to the floor with exhaustion. A few hours later, the dawn sun was pricking her eyes.

There was no sign of Salter. As she pulled on her clothes, through the window drifted the distant chime of a church bell. A single note, ringing low, joined by another and another. Moss couldn't help but be drawn to it and she leant out to listen. Soon the whole sky was filled with the sorrowful toll of bells. Below her, in the street, she saw people coming out of their houses. Though she couldn't make out what they said, she could see their faces were grave. Then she caught the murmur of their voices, drifting upwards.

'Queen Jane . . . childbed fever . . .'

When she saw them crossing themselves, she

understood. The sad bells rang for the passing of the Queen who'd given the King his son and heir. Who'd lain for two weeks with fever.

Jane Seymour was dead.

Moss tried to picture the baby prince, asleep in his cradle. The Lady Mary, kneeling in prayer. Little Elizabeth, scrunching up her berry-brown eyes to hold in her tears. Mothers all gone. When she thought of Elizabeth, too stubborn to pray like her sister, she felt sure her fierce spirit would find a way through. There was something extraordinary about the little girl with the battlefield curls. Moss wondered if she would ever see her again?

Pulling her head back inside the room, Moss jumped as the door opened. There was Salter, carrying a wooden platter. On it stood two bowls of steaming porridge, a pot of honey and a jug of cream.

'Breakfast!' he grinned and laid the platter on the floor. 'An' just in case yer wonderin, the Hollanders paid me good to work them herring boats.'

Moss flushed, remembering how she'd doubted him.

'I –'

'I know,' said Salter. He placed a warm bowl in her hands and his glance caught hers. Without any more words, she knew that he understood. Neither would forget what had happened between them. A friendship had been broken. But here, now, was something new.

It was the most delicious porridge she'd ever tasted. Moss scraped every dollop from the bowl then licked the creamy sweetness from her spoon.

'Good?' said Salter.

'Good.'

'Come on then. I've got something to show you.'

'What?'

'Wait and see.'

Moss followed him out of the tavern, down the little street that was already bustling to life, until they were at the river. When they reached the shingle, he stopped.

'Shut yer eyes,' said Salter.

'Really?'

'Go on. It's got to be a surprise.'

She hadn't a clue what Salter was up to, but whatever it was, she could see it was making him agitated: he was hopping from one foot to another with an edge of excitement to his voice.

Moss did as he asked. She felt him take her hand and lead her gently over the shore. She could hear the lap of waves growing louder and tasted the salt breeze on her lips. They were walking to the water's edge.

He stopped and squeezed her hand.

'Here,' he said, 'you can look now.'

She opened her eyes.

There in front of her, beached on the shore, was the most magical sight she had ever seen.

It was a boat. Nestling on the shingle, lit by the pink sun of the dawn. A boat garlanded with the silken-green leaves of trailing ivy. She could see the little vessel had been crafted from an odd assortment of wood and that it was unmistakably Salter's work. Woven with the soft leaves, it seemed to come from a place that was not London or the river, but a story.

'Oh. Salter . . .'

He looked at her and in the warmth of his gaze she felt as though she might laugh or cry or both.

A shy smile crept across Salter's face. 'Do you like it?'

'More than *anything*.'

He tugged the little boat across the shingle to the shallows. Then he held out his hand. 'Come with me then.'

She took his hand, stepping over the side and settling herself among the leaves in the bottom of the boat.

Salter pushed off from the shore and jumped in. He took the oars and pulled with deft strokes until they were mid-river.

Then he stopped rowing and let them drift for a few moments. All around them the silver-grey river sparkled to life. This river had brought them together. Without it, she would never have met Salter. Their fates were intertwined with the swirling, changing water. Moss had felt it inside her, felt the Riverwitch, powerful and vulnerable, the Witch's voice inside her head. The river was a part of her. *River Daughter*.

Salter was looking at her. She could see the crinkle of a smile coming, but there was something else too. It made her blink.

'Moss,' he said.

It was just a word, but to Moss it mattered. Her name. Not *Leatherboots*, the nickname that had caused so much trouble.

'Moss . . .'

In her heart the newness stirred. She couldn't place it. Like joy and grief bundled up together. It took her breath away.

His eyes remained fixed on hers, wide and brown in the glow of the morning sun.

'Where shall we go?' he said.

At that moment she realised she would go

anywhere. In that boat, with Salter. That whatever happened, she would not leave him. Just as the river was part of her, so too was Salter.

'Home?' he said.

'Home,' she replied.

She got up from the leaves and sat next to him, taking an oar in her hands. Together they rowed. And the river cradled the garlanded boat, the boy and the girl pulling with sure strokes. And it carried them back to where they'd begun – to the clear waters of the west.

A note from the author

History is an exciting place to go digging for stories. But when I read about a real life 'white bear' that had been kept at the Tower of London, along with lions, leopards, tigers, wolves, snakes and all manner of exotic creatures, I realised I'd stumbled upon something quite special. The bear was most likely a polar bear – a present from King Haakon of Norway to King Henry III of England in 1252. This dates it several hundred years before the white bear in my story. There are accounts of Henry III's bear being allowed to swim on the end of a chain and catch salmon in the River Thames – a nugget of history I couldn't resist thieving for a scene in the book. At this point, perhaps I should say that although there is much authentic historical detail in *River Daughter*, the world I've created is a fictional one. Real characters, events and places rub shoulders with a whole lot of things I've made up.

For anyone who wants to read more about the history of the animals kept in the Tower, I'd recommend Daniel Hahn's fascinating book, *The Tower Menagerie* or Geoffrey Parnell's *The Royal Menagerie at the Tower of London*. Of course the Tower of London has its own brilliant website with tales of the creatures that lived there. So if you ever get the chance to visit the Tower, you'll be able to imagine the roars of strange beasts rising over the battlements.

Jane Hardstaff

Acknowledgements

I would like to thank: the best agent a writer could have – Gillie Russell at Aitken Alexander; the editorially and generally brilliant Stella Paskins at Egmont; Andrea Kearney who perfectly imagined the world of Moss and brought two books to life with beautiful covers; Jenny Hayes, superbly gifted in the dark art of publicity; Hannah Sandford, unafraid to ask the tricky questions; Joe McLaren for his mesmerising chapter illustrations; wonderful booksellers Chris Ellis and Debby Guest from The White Horse Bookshop in Marlborough and Steven Pryse from Pickled Pepper Books in Crouch End; all those who read, reviewed, talked about and blogged about *The Executioner's Daughter*; Jean and Malcolm Hardstaff for *everything*; Frea, who named Jenny Wren and is always happy to talk about fighting girls; and Nick, whom I would not be without.